FLIP

By Briana Michaels

Copyright

All names, characters and events in this publication are fictitious and any resemblance to actual places, events, or real persons, living or dead, is entirely coincidental.

All rights reserved. No part of this publication may be reproduced, stored, or transmitted, in any form or by any means, without the prior permission, in writing, of the author.

www.BrianaMichaels.com

COPYRIGHT © 2022 Briana Michaels

Dedication

To all the dirty girls out there—
May your mascara run, lipstick smear, back arch,
and headboard break.
Be worshipped like the queen you are and settle
for nothing less.

Chapter 1

Trey

"Eyes on me, slut."

Erin's braced against the bathroom stall, her arms out wide, with her hands pressed on opposite walls. Her legs shake as she keeps them spread for me and rises on her tiptoes.

I love putting my girl on display. Especially when she cries as she comes hard.

Gripping her chin, I offer a partial smile while my fingers piston inside her wet pussy. She's so swollen and needy, the squelching noises alone have me nearly blowing my load in my pants. Fuck, she's stunning like this—flushed cheeks, messy hair, running mascara—it's a trifecta that always gets my dick hard.

"I can't. Oh god, I can't come again, Trey."

She can and she will.

I double down on my efforts and hit her g-spot harder. One of her heels falls off as she holds herself up and leans into my hand like she needs more.

Perfection.

"Keep looking at me," I demand as I lift her dress higher and squat down. Her scent smacks me in the face and my dick twitches. Finger-banging is fun, but sucking her clit is even better. Erin quakes, alternating between grunts and sobs when I drag my tongue across her cunt and give her swollen clit all the attention it deserves. I've made her come twice already, and this third one finally gives me the reward I seek.

Her eyes grow wide, her mouth opening in a silent scream when she detonates. Erin bursts into tears, gyrating against my face, but keeps her eyes on me just like I told her to. *Such a good girl.* I want that connection, that raw unraveling splendor. Her knees wobble and body sags as if she's just run a marathon. Rising to my feet again, I wrap one arm around her waist to hold her up and once her pussy finally stops squeezing my fingers, I pull out and lick her flavor off my lips.

"You're such a good little slut." I shove my fingers in her mouth. "Suck."

I want Erin to taste how good she is. I want her to know what it feels like to let loose, and what following orders like a good girl will get her.

Another sob wracks through her when I pull my digits from her mouth. "I… I don't know why… I'm crying." She sucks in ragged, labored breaths, and still grips the stall walls to hold herself upright. A few seconds tick by and she releases her position, and swipes her tears away, angrily.

Of course, she's mad. Erin gave herself permission to let go and this is the result: Three hard orgasms and smeared makeup.

It takes all I have not to run my thumb across her lips and smear that red lipstick all over her cheeks and chin. It also takes tremendous effort to not wipe the smudged mascara from her watery eyes.

I will. Trust me.

But first I want her to see what she looks like after surrendering.

"You did so good for me." Kissing her neck, I guide her towards the sink and press my chest against her back. I'm certain she can feel my hard cock dig into her ass. "Look how gorgeous you are."

Erin's face turns crimson, and eyes widen in shock as she gawks at her reflection. "Oh my god, Trey." She lurches forward and turns on the faucet, hurrying to wash that sex-induced look off of her beautiful face. "My makeup is destroyed."

In the best of ways.

I stand back and watch Erin grab a disposable hand towel to clean her face up with. Her hair has come undone too. Damn, she's perfection in a little black dress and I'm dying to rip that thing off her, bend her over this sink and blow her fucking back out. "You look amazing."

"I look like the conductor of the hot mess express."

And I wouldn't want her any other way.

Unable to keep my hands to myself, I brush the hair away from her shoulder to kiss it. Making sure to graze her with my teeth before licking her sweet skin, I start making my way towards her neck because I know it's her favorite erogenous zone.

"Trey."

"Hmm?" My lips trail down her shoulder blade as my hands ride up her ribcage. I palm her breasts through the fabric of her dress. Her tits are sensational.

Gripping the sink, her eyes flutter shut as I knead her tits in my big hands. "Trey, we've got to get it together."

The hell we do. "You in a hurry to escape me?" *Again*. I leave that last bit off because it's a sore topic for me still.

"Our dinner's probably getting cold."

"You ordered a salad."

"But Glitch…"

The mention of Glitch brings me to a stop. He's my best friend. He's also Erin's brother. And I'm breaking bro code by sneaking off with Erin like this.

Again.

Pulling back, I give her some breathing room while I count how many times I've gone behind my best friend's back to get what I want.

We're at this fancy restaurant because Glitch and his fiancé, Ara, want to celebrate their upcoming wedding with a nice, intimate dinner for just the bridal party and I abandoned them at the table to lure Erin in here for personal pleasure.

I was impressed I'd made it through putting in our dinner order before finding an excuse to get Erin in here. But now I feel like a jackass. Erin's right. Now isn't the time to push each other in fun ways.

This is the closest we've ever come to getting caught by her brother.

"Do you regret it?" I don't know what I'll do if she says yes. Erin could have told me to stop at any time and she hasn't. Ever. This isn't the first time we've snuck away to be together.

I just hope it won't be the last.

Sneaking around is her idea, not mine. I'm just desperate enough to take Erin however she'll let me. If the thrill of "almost getting caught" by someone is her thing, I'll embrace it. There's nothing I won't do for this woman.

Her lips are sealed tight, and she won't look at me. It makes my pulse race and stomach queasy. "Erin. Yes or no, do you regret what we're doing?"

"I don't want to do this with you right now."

Great, she's back to being captain of the ship. Erin's just used her mom voice on me, for fuck's sake. I watch as she finger-combs her long, dark hair before grabbing her purse from the vanity and pulls out lipstick. I bite the inside of my cheek as she applies a fresh coating of that deep red color I love on her so much. When she's happy with the cover-up from this little tryst, she turns around and looks at me.

I can't read the expression on her face. I've known this woman for nearly a decade but sometimes Erin seems like she's from a completely different planet. Makes sense considering all she's been through, but I'm sick of seeing her miserable every time I visit and the urge to do something about it has intensified lately.

Even as she flashes me a bright smile, all post-orgasm blissed out, Erin's happiness isn't convincing.

Good thing this night isn't over.

"When we sit down, I want you to order an appetizer."

She makes a what-the-fuck-face. "No."

I close the space between us and grab her chin. My thumb's poised to smear that lip color again. She sucks in a breath and holds it, locking her gaze with mine, daring me to do it. "You can't go all night drinking wine with only lettuce in your belly."

She arches her brow at me. "I'm a grown ass woman, Trey. Don't treat me like a child."

I just treated her like a whore, and she loved it. But when I try to take care of her outside of sex, she gets ten kinds of hostile with me, like her being three years older than me makes any difference in our power dynamic?

"For me," I say gently. "Drink water, and order something more substantial for me. *Please*."

She doesn't owe me a fucking thing. In fact, I half expect her to slap me across the face and walk out of here while I'm left behind with a raging hard-on.

"Why are you doing this?" she whispers.

"Because I care about you." There. I've said it.

Her brow pinches as if it's a foreign concept she can't grasp. "Trey. We can't do this again."

We can and we will.

She says this every time we hook up. And then when she sees me again, she drags me off to a dark corner and strips naked so I can have my way with her.

It started small. A kiss at first. Then it was a blowjob. Then it grew and grew until last Thanksgiving, I fucked her for hours then fed her half a pumpkin pie in bed afterwards. That night I grew an addiction. It's taken me months to corner this woman for another hit of the good stuff and I'll be damned if I waste a second of this opportunity. Her arousal is still in my nose and on my tongue. Even though she's giving me the cold shoulder right now, I know if I reach under her little black dress, I'll find her wet for me.

Erin's mouth opens slightly, her eyes heavy-lidded when I run my hands up her inner thighs. I let my fingers trail a soft path across her delectable skin and damn if she doesn't spread her legs to give me access to her pussy. Maybe she's as addicted to my touch as I am to hers.

Not that she'll ever admit it.

"Order something more to eat," I say, shoving my thick finger inside her again. I pull out and lick my finger clean while she watches. "Do as I say, or you'll be punished."

"Punished how?"

She matches my energy every time I bring it and I love that about this woman. But if she thinks she's the dominant one in our dynamic, she's mistaken. "I'll deny your orgasms."

Hand to the man, I think she's debating on risking it. But in the end, a small whimper slips from her pretty little mouth. "Okay."

I flash a victory smile and back away, snagging my suit jacket from the hook on the back of the door. Erin holds her hand out, waiting expectantly for something else.

I arch my brow and stare at her. "What?"

"Give them back."

Not a chance. "Oh, you mean these?" I pull her black silk panties out from my pants pocket. Dangling them from the finger I just fucked her with, I yank them away when she tries to grab them. "Nahhh, these belong to me now."

"Trey!" She has the cuteness to stomp her foot. "Please?"

"Better hurry." I dip down and kiss her neck. "Your brother's waiting for us to return."

Her attitude switches immediately.

"Yeah." Erin slips past me. "Better not keep your best friend waiting." She unlocks the door, swings it open, and stomps out of the restroom.

My stomach drops. "Fuck." I went too far, haven't I?

Slamming my fists on the vanity, I glare at my reflection and barely recognize myself. I'm a shit person. I shouldn't be messing around with Erin. But how can I not? She's incredible. Strong. Independent.

And she deserves someone who cares about her.

I'm that someone, damnit, whether I should be or not.

Closing my eyes, all I picture is her round green eyes staring at me while she comes over and over from my touch. I pull her panties back out of my pocket and bring them to my nose.

Fuuuuuck.

She'll be my undoing.

Erin's the kind of woman the devil himself would crawl out of Hell and be a better man for. She should be worshipped, spoiled, protected at all costs.

And fucked six ways to Sunday.

The thought makes me smile. When am I going to get a chance to see her again after this? We only hang when I'm in town visiting Glitch, and I'm not sure if that's my doing or hers. Meeting like this, on the sly, in group settings, seems to be the only time she lets herself be with me.

I both hate and love it.

After stuffing Erin's panties back in my pocket, I put my jacket on and straighten my tie. Time to go back out there and behave.

I quickly join the rest dinner party and take my seat next to Erin at the table. Except she isn't there. "Where's Erin?"

Glitch frowns. "She's sick."

What? No, she's not. "Where'd she go?"

Ara glances at Glitch before turning to me. "Home."

God. Damnit. Erin's not sick, she's faking it because she feels ashamed about what we just did. I'm not letting that happen. But I don't know how to get out of this dinner so I can chase her down.

My heart's racing a mile a minute as I try to figure a way out of this. The waitress brings us our dinner and sets Erin's salad down at her empty seat before placing my plate in front of me. I'm torn between bolting and playing it cool. The last thing I want to do is eat the filet mignon I ordered.

"Poor Erin." Ara leans back in her chair and wipes her mouth with a napkin. "I hope it's nothing too serious."

I hate that they're worried for her when I know the truth.

I hate that I'm going to sit here and celebrate without Erin when she should be here enjoying this dinner with us. It's an important night.

I need a drink.

No, I need to get the fuck out of here and go get my girl.

"Can I get you anything else?"

Glitch smiles at the waitress. "Not for me. Ara?"

"I'm good."

I'm not. "Can I get a Jack and coke, please?"

Once it arrives, I lift my glass and toast my best friend and his beautiful bride-to-be. "To love," I say. "May it never slip between your fingers." *Or out the restroom door.* "Cheers, you two. It's about fucking time."

I no sooner clank my glass with my two friends when I feel a clock start ticking in my heart.

Erin's not a fling. She's a forever. If I don't play my cards right, I'll not only lose the woman I've fallen in love with but also my best friend.

I can't let either of those things happen.

"Excuse me, guys." I'm on my feet before I even realize it. "I gotta go."

Chapter 2

Erin

Stupid, stupid, stupid. I should have never met Trey in that bathroom. This is all my fault. The way I feel. The way my mind is spinning. I can't believe I let myself do unspeakable things in a public bathroom with that man.

And I can't believe how much I loved it.

I don't understand what's going on with us. This isn't the first time we've hooked up and, damnit, I don't want it to be the last. It should be though. Trey deserves a woman who has her shit together.

I'm a single mom with no job and no life. The only time I have fun is with my brother and Ara, and those times usually include Trey because he's like family at this point too. We've known each other since Glitch went to MIT and brought Trey home on break.

We hit it right off.

Things were cool for so long—I'd low key crush on a guy who had a bright future, he'd playfully engage in fun conversations until he somehow became part of our tiny family.

Then two years ago we kissed.

And that's when things got all messed up.

Beeeep. I lay on the horn and scream, "A blinker would be nice, asshat!" Speeding around the jerk in front of me, I flip him off and finally make my way out of the big city. I hate crowds. I hate peopling.

I hate that I don't have my panties on.

What's Trey going to do with them anyway? Why keep them for any reason other than to make me feel ashamed for degrading me in the bathroom like that.

Wait. Do I feel ashamed and degraded? Kinda.

Fine. No. Not really. I like that he stuffed them in his pocket as a keepsake. What I don't like, is how I'm already tallying up how many pairs of panties I have in my drawer so I can encourage him to do it again.

Holy crap, what is wrong with me? This needs to stop.

Trey's hot as fuck and charismatic to a fault. He could charm underwear off a nun if he wanted. I'm not far off from being a holy sister at this point. Trey's the only man I've let myself be with in over two years. Before that, my love life was dismal and nearly obsolete. Ever since I had my son, I don't let men into my life easily.

Honestly, I'm shocked I don't have cobwebs between my legs.

It's not that I haven't tried dating, because believe me, I have. But with my work schedule and Beetle being the center of my life, I've never had time for bullshit dates and booty calls. Besides, most guys see that I have a nine-year-old kid and run the other way.

My heart sinks a little thinking of Beetle. I miss him.

Pulling up to our house, all the lights are off, and it makes my heart sink a little coming home to an empty house. Beetle's away at camp and will be for much of the summer. I hate when he's not here to drive me crazy. But I'm glad he's experiencing fun things and hopefully making new friends.

Heading inside, I kick off my shoes, flick on the lights, and sigh. It's good to be home. This is the only house I've ever lived in and I'm not sure if that's a good or bad thing. Running upstairs, I quickly get out of my dress and put on a pair of pajama pants and a loose-fitting t-shirt with Ghostface on it. It's nice to dress up for a night, but it's a million times better to eat junk food and horror movies in comfort.

My stomach growls.

Too tired to make something decent, I trudge into the kitchen and dump cereal in a bowl before plopping on the couch. I no sooner find the remote when my doorbell rings.

Don't answer it. Pretend you're not home.

I'm not expecting company so whoever it is can fuck right off.

"Erin?" Trey's voice booms, hitting me square in the chest.

Shit, shit, shit! I get up so fast, milk and cereal slosh all over my hands. "Trey? What are you doing here?"

"You really need to keep your door locked."

"You really need to not walk into people's houses."

"You didn't answer when I rang the bell."

I want to say a lot of things—mostly about how I didn't want to answer because I'm not in the mood for company. But my bitchy attitude evaporates when I see him standing in the foyer with a huge paper bag.

"Why are you here?"

"Glitch said you were sick."

We both know it's a lie, so I don't say anything. Trey walks further into my house and drops the bags of food on the dining table. Without saying a word, he heads to the kitchen and grabs plates, cups, and silverware.

"What are you doing?" I don't understand him at all.

"We were supposed to have dinner tonight."

"Yeah, well, plans change."

"Exactly." He pulls out box after box after box of food. "I went ahead an ordered extra. Figured leftovers are never a bad thing to have in the fridge—especially considering how busy the next couple of days will be. I also swung by that taco place Beetle likes and bought him guac and chips for when he gets home from camp."

Tears threaten to spill, but I refuse to allow it. My entire body sags instead. "Why are you doing this?"

Trey pops the lid off the salad I'd ordered at the restaurant and starts scooting it onto a plate. "You left before you could eat."

"I'm aware. And I'm already eating." Holding up my bowl of cereal makes me feel childish, but I can't seem to pull it together. Trey coming here like this is weird. And wonderful. "We don't do things together without Glitch."

He stops what he's doing and flashes me a huge smile. "I think we've done plenty of things together without Glitch."

"You know what I mean." I'm walking towards him like the smell of gourmet food and Trey's cologne are luring me in.

He doesn't say a word while he finishes plating our dinner. "Sit down, Erin."

Fuck that. I glower at him instead.

I'm mad and confused and touched all at the same time. It's always like this with Trey. My pride and heart get too confused.

He sits down and pours us each a glass of wine.

Oh my God, he even picked up a bottle of my favorite Riesling. I can't with this man.

I'd be a jerk if I didn't sit with him and eat, right? I might not have asked for it, but the gesture is incredibly thoughtful. And I know why I'm struggling to sit and enjoy this meal.

I don't know how to be taken care of.

Is that what Trey's trying to do? I can't even tell. The concept is so far gone from my norm, I legit can't figure out what to say or do right now.

Leaning back in his chair, he stares at me with a stern expression, waiting for me to make up my mind. Running his gaze up and down my body, he says, "There's a Scream marathon tonight."

Damn him for knowing all my weaknesses. I drop into my chair and pick up my fork. Without saying another word, I stab my lettuce and shove a forkful in my mouth. It's good, but I'd rather have the steak Trey's carefully carving a piece off of on his plate. "Can I try that?"

He watches me carefully. I can feel his eyes burning my skin, heating me down to my core.

"Open that pretty mouth for me." He stabs a hunk of meat, lifts his fork to my mouth and feeds me. It's the most intimate thing we've done apart from the pumpkin pie episode last Thanksgiving.

"That's really good."

Trey carves off another piece and feeds me that too.

I refuse to take a third bite and stop him. "You enjoy it. I only wanted a taste. Glitch always raves about that place and their steaks, but I've never been."

Trey sips his wine and then loads his fork with a piece of steak, a carrot, and a little sauce. "They're worried about you," he says before stuffing his mouth.

God, even the way he chews is sexy. His jawline is stupidly hot and don't get me started on his mouth.

Or what his mouth can do…

"I'll text them later and tell them I feel fine."

"Why'd you run, Erin?"

I sit back in my chair and stare at him. "Like you don't know?"

"No. I don't know. That's why I'm asking. Because it can't be that you felt shame for what we did. It can't be because you have no idea how to compose yourself after coming hard under my tongue. And it's not because you suddenly got the flu."

He's right. "I'm…" What can I say? "I'm confused and didn't want to be a drag at dinner."

"One, you're never a drag, so get that notion out of your head. Two, what are you confused about?"

I deadpan him.

He takes another bite of his steak, unaffected. "That look won't work on me. Use your words, Erin."

How dare he talk to me like this! "I think you should leave."

Trey doesn't budge. "Not until we've come to an agreement."

"An *agreement*?" What did that even mean?

"No more games, Er."

"You fingering me in the bathroom wasn't a game. You eating my pussy wasn't a game. We don't play games, Trey."

"You being hot and cold with me is a fucking game." He drops his fork and knife, and they clank loudly on his plate. "If I asked you out to dinner, what would you say?"

"I'd say you already brought dinner here so there's no point."

"What about tomorrow night?"

"You bought food for then too." Look at this spread! He knows what he's done. He said it himself, tons of leftovers, on purpose.

"The night after?"

"Beetle will be back, and I don't have a babysitter."

"He can come with us."

My anger rises and I don't even know why. "Why are you doing this?"

He stands up and my heart pounds in my chest. He turns my chair, with my ass still planted in it, and grips the sides of the seat by my thighs. His mouth is super close to mine and his eyes have gold flecks in them under this lighting. "I want you, Erin."

"You had me."

He shakes his head. "Not talking about on the sly in a bathroom, or in a pantry, or in your motherfucking laundry room."

Oh yeah… the laundry room. How did I forget that time in the laundry room where he ate me out until I lost all brain function?

"I'm talking about for keeps."

Keeps? Oh hell no. He needs to leave. Now. "I'm tired, I'm going to bed."

Trey doesn't back away, but I know he won't keep me trapped either. If I wanted up, he'd move. I just haven't budged.

"Give us a try, Erin." He presses his mouth softly to mine and my head spins with a million ways this could blow up in my face. Trey's important to me. He's even more important to Beetle. If this doesn't work out, I'm not the only one who will feel the pain. Relationships are work. They require time and attention, and I don't have the capacity for it.

"I'm…" *Scared.* "I'm tired, Trey. Please leave." I push up and he leans back, giving me some space to move around.

"Fine." His defeated tone makes me whimper. With his head down, he leaves my house and says, "Lock the door behind me, please."

My heart collapses when the front door clicks shut.

Chapter 3

Trey

"Wait!"

I stop at the bottom of Erin's porch steps and slowly turn around. She's clinging to the doorjamb hard enough to suggest she's using it to hold herself up. I stare up at her. If she wants me to stay, she'll have to use her words and tell me exactly what she wants from me.

Erin never seems to do what she wants, only what everyone else wants. I'm not sure if she's ever done something for herself. So I wait.

And I wait.

And I wait.

"Trey…"

"Yes, Erin?"

She swallows hard and my dick twitches. "Stay the night?"

There it is. Finally, she's letting herself take something she wants. And I'm so glad it's me. "Are you asking or telling me?"

She shrugs and gives me a sheepish grin. "Both, I guess."

My feet hit the steps one thud at a time as I close the distance between us. Then I run my hand along the underside of her jaw and cup her face. "You sure?"

"Mmm hmm."

I lean down and press my mouth to hers in a gentle but controlling kiss. With our mouths fused, I back her sweet ass up and maneuver us into her small foyer. At six-foot-four, I tower over Erin in a dominating way I intend to use to make her fall to her knees. Often. She's so strong, so independent and capable, I'm going to have to pull out every weapon in my arsenal to get her to open up for me.

The top of her head hits my chin, but her attitude makes her seem ten feet tall. She's earned every fucking inch and all of my respect long ago. Having her turn to putty in my hands is something I've craved since I first met her. But I haven't tried to master it until two years ago when I first kissed her exactly like how I'm kissing her now.

Erin needs to feel safe enough to let people in. She's been in charge for so long, giving up control isn't easy for her. But I think it's necessary to have balance in life.

She digs her nails into the back of my neck, moaning as she deepens our kiss. My hungry hands glide down the slope of her waist until I cup her perfectly round ass. She squeaks when I lift her up and automatically wraps her legs around me. It's like an animal inside me unleashes and I slam her against the wall. I break away from her mouth to kiss her neck where she likes.

"Fuuck." She scrapes my scalp with her nails. "Trey, I…"

"Tell me what you want." It's hers. Whatever it is, I'll make sure she gets it.

"I… I want…"

I have a feeling she wants so much right now, she's not sure what to ask for first. That's okay. We have all night. Hell, if I had my way, we'd have the rest of our lives to make her fantasies come true. But I've got to take this one step at a time. She spooks easily.

"How about we finish dinner first?"

My suggestion catches her off guard.

"Oh." She unhooks her legs from my waist and slides down. "Umm. Okay."

I lift her chin with my finger and arch my brow. "I want you filled to the brim, Erin. Food and water first. Then my dick. If I'm spending the night, I sure don't expect either of us to get any sleep, and for what I have planned, you're going to need all the energy you can get."

So will I.

Her cheeks blaze red. Her pupils blow wide. "Well then." She lets out a little laugh and my heart swells with the sound of it. "I guess I better hydrate."

"Definitely."

I back off just enough for her to have some wiggle room, but her body still has to brush mine to slip past me. Following her into the dining room, I stare at her plump ass and almost regret putting a pause to our make-out session. But she needs to eat and drink. I wasn't kidding about that.

Erin looks over her shoulder at me and tosses a smile that hits my heart. This woman goes through emotions like weebs go through anime—several at once. She's chaotic and controlled. Methodical. Messy.

I love her.

Shit. Nope. Not going there. The L word is not on the table.

Erin's my best friend's sister and falling in love with her would put a catastrophic hole in my friendship with Glitch. It might also put a gigantic roadblock in my personal plans.

"Not there," I say as Erin goes to her chair. "Here." I sit in my seat and tap my leg. "I want you right here, my hungry little slut."

The air whooshes out of her. I hold my breath to see if she's going to play along and obey or throw her plate of food at me. Imagine my elation when she straddles my thighs. "Such a good girl." I grab a handful of her hair and tug it enough to make her lean back so I can kiss the pulse point on her throat. Reaching around her, I slide her plate over and move my own meal out of the way. "Eat for me."

She doesn't. Her shoulders sag and she stares at the spread of food with her hands clenched closed in her lap. This isn't going to work. Maybe she's struggling to take orders from someone else. Maybe she's rethought her meal choice.

Maybe she's regretting asking me to stay.

I snake my hand around her middle and bury my way into her pants. She sucks in a little gasp. "So wet," I rumble against her ear. "Be a good girl for me and eat something. I'll make you wetter with every bite you take." I apply a little pressure to her clit and circle my middle finger on it when she reaches for her fork. "That's a good girl. Take a bite for me."

She stabs a piece of my steak.

Fuuuck, I love this so much.

Erin can take anything she needs from me—my time, my dick, my dinner, my heart. I just want her cared for in every way.

She groans while chewing. Her pleasure could be from the flavor of the meat… or from the way I've just increased the speed of my finger on her clit. Her head falls back on my shoulder while she chews. "So good."

I dip my finger into her cunt, relishing how slick she is. "Keep going, Erin. Clean the fucking plate." I start rubbing her clit again while she takes another bite.

"This is... such a... a good... pairing. Fuuuck." She grunts and has to put down her glass of wine before I make her spill it.

I plunge two fingers into her sweet pussy, curling them as much as I can to hit her g-spot from this angle. "Did I say you could stop?" I gather her hair in my freehand and pull. "Now eat some of the veggies."

Her pussy clenches around my fingers. She's wetter now. I can feel a spot forming on my thigh.

"This is crazy," she says, breathlessly. Doesn't stop her from plucking a carrot off my plate and devouring it though.

She takes another sip of the wine and I pull my fingers out of her pussy. "Open your mouth, little slut."

She looks over her shoulder at me, her brow furrowed. I don't repeat myself because I know damn well she heard me the first time. Erin drops her mouth open, and I shove my fingers inside it. "Suck them clean like a good little whore for me."

Erin's practically buzzing in my lap at this point. Once she's sucked her taste off my fingers, I shove the plates away and lift her off my lap. In a swift motion, I have her ass planted on the table and am working her pajama pants off. God damn, she's spectacular. How can a woman look so fucking delicious in a pair of baggy, cotton pants with penguins all over them?

Don't get me going on her oversized t-shirt.

I pull her pants down, happy to see she's cooperating beautifully. Sitting back in my chair, I pin her ankles at the sides of my thighs and stare at her, spread open, half naked, and not taking charge for once. I love how she goes along with what I want her to do. I love that she trusts me enough to let her guard down.

Erin's cheeks are still flushed but her shoulders have rolled back. My girl feels powerful like this.

As she should.

Stabbing another big hunk of my steak, she holds her fork out to me. "Want some?"

"If you think that's the meal I intend to devour, Erin, you've forgotten who you've invited back into your house."

Her laugh is music to my ears. "I don't compare to an entrée of this caliber."

"Are you comparing yourself to a steak?"

She shrugs and eats the bite herself. "Maybe."

I'm mad, but I try to not let it show. How dare she compare herself to something so basic. Erin's a luxury no man on earth but me can enjoy. "Finish off my plate."

"It's yours. I've eaten more than I should already."

A well-placed slap on her pussy makes her yelp. "I said eat."

"Trey!"

"*Eat.*" I slap her there again.

She sucks in a deep breath and her thighs quiver. "I'll… I'll eat if you eat."

Fuck me sideways. "You aren't in a position to give orders or make negotiations."

"On the contrary," she says with a big smile. "I'm in the prime position to give orders and make negotiations." She closes her legs and opens them again. Open, close, open, close.

Fucking tease.

But she's not wrong and I'm thrilled she knows her place in this dynamic. I might get her to melt like butter when I call her my dirty little slut, but Erin needs to always remember who's in charge — her.

I slide my hands between her closed thighs and pry them open easily. With my gaze locked on hers, I lean down and drag my tongue along her slick folds. Her pussy is swollen and ripe for eating. I slap it again, not too hard, not too soft, and say, "Clean that fucking plate, slut." Then I seal my mouth over her cunt and feast.

She stays firmly seated on the edge of the table, spread eagle, and I hear the faint sounds of her fork stabbing things on a plate while blood rushes to my dick. It's so hard, the zipper of my suit pants is cutting into me. I use that biting pain to stay grounded. I'm close to shredding her shirt off and fucking her recklessly on this dining table and I don't want to unleash myself yet.

Doubling down, I finger and tongue fuck her, alternating speeds until I find the right combo that makes Erin come undone. Her taste floods my mouth. Her pussy clenches down on my finger and I'm in heaven.

"Trey!"

I lift my head at the sound of my name on her sweet lips and…

Lose. Control.

I shove the plates away. Some crash onto the floor. I pull Erin's oversized shirt over her head and immediately suck on the first thing I can get my mouth on. Her nipples are big. I love them. Dragging my tongue in large circles around her breast, I graze my teeth and bit down just enough to make her hiss through clenched teeth. Looking up, I read her expression and see she's part shocked and hella into it.

Fuck. Yes.

I reach up and pinch her other nipple, rolling it between my thumb and forefinger, tugging it a little.

"Oh my god." Erin grabs the back of my head and holds me in place while I suck in as much of her breast as I can into my mouth. This girl is plenty more than a handful. They're soft, heavy…

And I'd say neglected.

That's about to change. "I'm going to fuck your tits and come all over them."

She laughs and leans back to give me access to her neck next. "Better make them slippery for you then, huh?"

My naughty girl grabs the remaining glass of wine and dumps it all over her chest.

I lap up the Riesling, taking my time to clean off every drop, then I sit back in my seat again and glance at the only plate left on the table. It's mine. Or… what's left of it. Like a good girl, she's eaten her meal, and just like I promised, I ate mine as well. But we're far from done.

"What happened to fucking my tits?"

"Earn it first." I snatch the plate and balance in it the palm of my hand. "Clean. The plate."

Erin tenses.

"Lick it, slut. Don't leave a drop left behind. I certainly didn't waste any of that wine on you."

I keep reading her cues, both verbal and non-verbal, to make sure I'm not taking this too far with her tonight. But when Erin leans forward, and she drags her pink tongue all over the dish, I know we're all good.

Holy. Hell.

"That's a good girl." I set the plate down and lean forward to show her how good sluts who listen get rewards. Shoving my finger in her pussy again, I drag it along the pad of flesh in there that makes her breath turn ragged within seconds. Then I add a second finger and suck on her clit while I annihilate her good senses.

"*Trey!*"

Erin's thighs clamp around my head, and she bucks off the table. It's a hell of a ride and I've only just started. Once I wring two orgasms from her this way, I help her off the table, and make of show of licking her cream off my mouth.

Placing my hand on her head, I force her to her knees. "You've been such a good little slut for me, Erin. I think you should have your dessert now."

I pull my cock out, and the instant it's free, I sigh with relief. It was starting to lose circulation in my pants. I see her eyes widen the instant she notices my new jewelry.

"Wow."

"You like?" I sure hope so, because I got this ladder with her in mind.

"I… ummm…. *Wow*." Erin traces her fingertips across the bars. There are nine total. One for every inch I'm dying to give her tonight.

I close my eyes when she flicks her tongue out to explore me with her mouth. "My dirty girl likes taking this big cock, don't you?"

"Mmmph." She swallows my head easily enough, but the rest will be harder for her.

I'm hung. I know this. I also know how intimidating it can be for a woman to be with someone my size. Erin's up for the challenge every time. She pulls back and looks at my dick again then licks it. "This feels wild."

No, it feels like I'm going to blow my load if she keeps doing that thing to the underside of my dick.

"More sucking, less talking. Or do you not want your dessert?"

I see her battle with liking and hating how I talk to her. She tests me by looking away at the mess we've made around us. Food, plates, wine… it's all over the hardwood floor. "Eyes on me, Erin." I'll be damned if she's going to falter now.

Erin flicks her gaze up to meet mine, her long black lashes framing two emerald, green eyes that I could drown myself in. I almost cave. I almost confess. I almost tell her everything I've been keeping inside me for far too long.

But she opens her mouth and wraps those luscious lips around my dick, and I forget the English language entirely. She sucks me off like she's trying to coax my fucking soul out through the head of my cock. I think she succeeds because when I'm close, I grab the back of her head and start saying shit I'm not calibrating right. "That's it, pretty little slut. Swallow everything I pump into you, like a greedy fucking whore on her knees."

She grabs my balls and squeezes them while working her hot mouth and freehand on my shaft. My heart's pounding. Heat blooms across the back of my neck. "Gonna come so hard down your throat." I pump into her mouth, rocking my hips a little, forcing her to choke on me. "Let me hear you gag."

Erin gurgles and slurps and chokes on me while drool drips off her chin and all over her chest.

Perfection.

I pull her off me by tugging on her hair and almost come when she fights me for more dick in her mouth instead of the air I'm trying to give her. Stepping back, I take over where I've forced her to leave off and stroke my cock hard and brutally. The piercings run along my hand, her spit's dripping down my length, and she's sitting so pretty on her knees, eyes watery, lashes clumped, and mouth wide open for me.

"You want this, filthy girl?"

She keeps her mouth open, tongue out like a target, and nods eagerly.

Bracing myself against the table, I nearly drive her backwards pushing my dick back into her mouth. "Push your tits together for me."

Erin obeys, and I spread my legs as much as I can for still having pants on. I lose my breath. I can't see clearly. I can't think straight. I pull out of her mouth and stuff my cock between her tits. Holy shit, I can't believe she's letting me use her body for my pleasure like this. "Open your mouth for me."

She does and I stuff my cock inside it again until I hit the back of her throat. She gags and I see stars. "Fuck yeah, baby. Choke on me."

When she runs her fingers along my taint, I bark something incoherent and start sweating. I'm trying to hold out for as long as possible, but my Kryptonite presents itself the instant Erin stares up at me with tears and smeared mascara dripping down her cheeks.

My body explodes.

I pull back and stroke myself as cum shoots out in thick, white jets, covering her face, her tits, her tongue. I took a beautiful thing and made it even more breathtaking. Stumbling back, I suck in ragged breaths as stars twinkle in my vision. My fucking ears are ringing.

Erin runs a hand down her face to wipe off my cum and then she licks her hand clean.

Holy. Shit.

I'm on her in an instant. Cushioning her head, I lower my girl onto her back and kiss every bit of skin I touch. "I want to fuck you, Erin."

Her pulse races wildly in her neck. I wait for a response that doesn't seem like it's coming. "It's okay to say no."

"Do… you have a condom?"

"No. Do you?"

She shakes her head. "I can't fuck you without one, Trey. That's a deal breaker."

"I know." I sit back on my haunches and try to regain a little composure. I packed an entire box of condoms with me, but they're at the hotel. I didn't plan to come to Erin's tonight. I figured she'd come back with me to the hotel. To say that now seems like a moot point. "Well then…" I run a hand over my head and mask my disappointment with a smile. "Guess we'll have to wait on that."

Erin rolls over, and I swear there's a chill coming off her. "It was fun while it lasted. I need to clean this up anyway."

Before she can grab the first dish on the floor, I stop her. "This mess can wait. I'm not even close to being finished with you yet."

"But we don't have any condoms."

"I don't need one for what I want to do."

"But…"

I cock my brow. "You want to call it quits now?"

She looks away. "No. But…"

"Stop with the buts." I lift her into my arms and make my way towards the stairs. "I'm not in town for long, I'd like to make the most of it with you before we have another long break."

The words are sad as they leave my mouth. Truth be told, I don't want a break from Erin. And I'm scared to tell her that because she'll likely bolt. In all the years I've known this woman, she's never had a boyfriend. As far as I know, she rarely even has hookups. Outside of me, anyway.

I hope.

Fuck, just thinking about another man touching her has me wanting to burn the world down.

I know after this wedding is over, it'll be another long break before Erin will want to see me again and I fucking hate it.

Nudging her bedroom door open with my foot, I slip inside and don't bother to turn on the lights. Lowering Erin onto her bed, I try to figure out what I should and shouldn't say tonight.

"Trey?"

"Hmmm?"

"I'm sorry."

"There's nothing for you to be sorry about."

"I should have been prepared."

No. *I* should have been prepared. But that would require me to also be presumptuous. "You were prepared for dinner, which was all this was supposed to be tonight. Neither one of us planned to make it back to your house to fuck."

My mood is souring, and I'm mad at myself for it.

"I should have though," she says, following me into her bathroom.

I make sure to maintain eye contact while I start the shower for her. "Should have what?"

"Known we'd make it to this point." Erin leans against the sink, relaxed, naked, and hair all disheveled. She still has some of my cum on her cheek. "We've been working our way here for a long time."

Not as long as I've been in love with you. "You always said sex was off the table—except for that one time. I didn't think you'd change your mind."

"Yes, you did. Otherwise, you wouldn't still come around."

Now I'm really pissed off. Does she think I only want to bang her? Fuck that. I bite back my temper because honestly, she's not entirely wrong. I brought condoms for a reason. I'd hoped we could take it to that level again while I'm in town, but that doesn't mean I was planning on it.

"I thought we had an understanding. My persistence has only ever been to push you deeper into your kinks, Erin. And mine."

"What about last Thanksgiving?"

"What about it?"

"We fucked then."

Like she has to remind me of the greatest night of my life? "And you said it was a one-off."

"You brought condoms to your hotel."

"For a precaution in case you changed your mind." I dip my head down to get in her face, so she sees how serious I am. "I'm just covering all bases to make sure you have whatever you need."

Erin starts closing up on me. "Things have changed."

"Changed how?"

She stares at me for a long moment and then shrugs and walks away from me.

Chapter 4

Erin

I almost slip and tell Trey that what's changed is that I have big, deep feelings for him. And where will that land me?

No. Where will that land *him*?

Trey's been the only man I've even let touch me in a long time. Not that he knows about my non-existent love life, and I'm not willing to share my secrets or bare my soul to him any time soon.

I should have been prepared for tonight. I know that. Even if it was a waste of money and we didn't fuck, at least I should have planned for it and stashed condoms in my room.

Because ever since we fucked, it's all I think about when I'm alone at night in my bed. And in the shower. Even when I'm gardening…

Wow, I'm pathetic. I'm also out of my depth.

Trey looks at me like I'm the hottest woman on earth. Spoiler alert: I'm not.

My ass is starting to sag, my boobs were never the same after I had my son, and I've been running myself to the ground for years. I can't remember the last time I got a decent night's sleep. Shit, I can't even remember the last time I had my eyebrows waxed.

I rub my eyes and realize I still have some of Trey's cum on my damn face.

Holy crap. I'm a mess.

No. I'm a dumpster fire.

Trey should run, fast and far from me if he knows what's good for him.

The alternative is having him stay forever, and that's not going to happen. He's got his career, a social life, adventure and excitement. A golden path of success is laid out before him, and I'd only be a roadblock. A dead end. There's no way I'd ever want to stop him from going after all he wants and Trey's the kind of man who would not only hang the moon for his woman, but he'd also shut down the world so she could take a break and relax while he did all the heavy lifting.

He's perfect.

"You coming, or am I going to have to put you over my shoulder and fireman carry you in here, Erin?"

He's also bossy, did I mention that?

I like it though. It's nice to give in and let someone else take the reins for a night. Trey's the only one I've ever submitted to. I try to not think about why that might be.

He meets me at the doorway to the bathroom and wraps his massive hands around my waist. "There you are," he says. "Thought you'd snuck off to clean the mess downstairs."

I should have.

As if he can't tell my heart is cracking, Trey flashes me a brilliant smile and ushers me into my own shower. He closes the curtain and leaves me alone for a few heartbeats before joining me. Thank god. I think I'd cry if he didn't.

I'm not sure where we stand with each other. Tonight escalated for us in more than one way — at least on my end. Yes, I want to have sex with him again. Yes, I want him to stay for however long I can convince him to.

But my son will be home from camp in a couple days, and what on earth would I tell him about Trey being here? Or worse… Glitch? He'll kill me if he knows I've been hooking up with his best friend. Keeping secrets from each other is not how we generally work. In fact, it was a rule I put in place right after our parents died. I couldn't bear the thought of Glitch going through anything — good or bad — and me not being a part of it. Now I'm keeping this huge thing from him, and it feels wrong.

This is getting serious.

Sometimes I imagine what life with Trey would look like. I squash it before getting too far though. It only hurts to think of it.

Trey takes up all the space and air in my little shower. He's a big guy. Chiseled body, dark brown eyes, full lips, amazing personality — he's the complete fantasy package, and he knows it. Oh I've seen the way he swaggers into a room. Sometimes his confidence rubs off on me. It only lasts as long as our trysts, but I love every second of how he makes me feel.

"Thank you," he says, cupping my face.

It takes me a second to realize he's wiping cum off my cheek. "For the best blow job ever?"

His laugh warms my skin more than the shower does. "For that, and also for trusting me enough to push you like this… *dirty girl*."

The pleasure, I sometimes fear, is all mine. I snatch my loofa and body wash, then busy myself because I don't want to talk anymore.

"Here, let me." Trey plucks the loofa from my hand and turns me around, scrubbing my back first.

He does a thorough job of cleaning every inch of my backside, and even squats down and kiss both my butt cheeks before rising to his full height again. "Goddamn," he says, slapping my ass. The sound is loud in the steamy bathroom. I swear I feel his handprint burning into my skin.

I wish it would.

"I could eat you for breakfast, lunch, and dinner." He spins me around and starts working on my front. Making wide circles around each of my breasts, he looks enthralled while I stand there, unsure of what to do with my hands. I grab shampoo.

"I wanted to do that next," he fusses.

"Well, my water heater sucks, which means we've got about two more minutes of hot water left so… maybe next time."

Will there be a next time? God, I hope so.

Trey pulls the nozzle down and sprays the soap off me from head to toe. True to its nature, my water starts cooling before he's rinsed my feet off.

"Shit, you weren't lying." Trey starts spraying himself off, and I see goosebumps rise along his skin. His nipples harden and muscles tense up because now the water is near frigid. "Woo! That'll wake you up."

I laugh even though I'm partially embarrassed. I can't even offer him a long hot shower. How could I possibly offer him a life with me and my son?

Stepping out of the shower, I give him a fresh, dry towel from my cabinet. "You should probably go."

"What happened to me staying?"

"I need to get some sleep. There's a lot to get done before the wedding."

"I'm here to help."

"Glitch will be here early in the morning. He can't know you spent the night."

"Erin. We can't keep doing this."

We have to, because once we stop it's over. "I'm not ready to make a change yet."

"Says the woman who just finished telling me things have changed."

Damnit. He's right. I'm being stupid. No grown ass woman should act like this. "Look, maybe you should…"

"I'm not leaving."

My heart thuds hard in my throat. "Trey."

"Erin." He dries off and hangs his towel. Standing in front of me… no, *towering* in front of me, he licks his lips, and his expression turns somber. "Look, I'm gonna be straight with you. I don't like that we just hook up when I'm in town. I don't like that I have to wait for an excuse to see you when I want to be able to call you whenever I want and swing by to pick you up so we can spend time together."

"Swing by," I scoff. "You live over two hours away. You can't just swing by."

"I'm not finished with what I have to say."

His authoritative tone shuts me up, and that's never happened before.

"You're not just some challenge for me, Erin. You're more than that. So yeah, I guess things have changed. On both our ends. If you don't want to see where this thing between us can go, then tell me now. But if you're willing to give me a shot... *a real shot*... then let me into your life as more than this." He flicks his hands between our naked bodies. "I lo—" Trey clears his throat and tries again. "I love being with you. And Beetle. I love how we are together."

"You mean you love having a slut on her knees with your cock in her mouth and cum on her face." I fold my arms to hug myself. I'm picking a fight, and I know it, but can't seem to stop. It's this or hear him confess something I'm not ready to hear.

Or worse, be let down because he's not going to confess what I'm not ready to hear.

Jesus, I'm a clusterfuck.

"You're right." Trey clenches his molars, making his jaw sharper. "I like having you on your knees for me." He drops to floor and says, "And I love being on mine for you."

I swear I feel faint. This topic is shifting again, and I can't find my bearings. "Get up."

"Not until I'm done saying what I have to say."

Then say it before I unravel and make a fool out of myself. "Fine."

"Go to dinner with me."

"We just did that!"

"I mean after the wedding. With Beetle. Just the three of us."

I back up and throw my hands out. "Whoa, whoa, whoa."

Trey rises to his feet. "We've done it before."

"That didn't count! Glitch was there too."

"So?"

"So?" What does he mean *so*? "So, my son will be there with us. He might get the wrong impression."

"And what would that be, Erin? That a man wants to take his mother out for a nice night? That he might see someone treat his mother like a fucking queen for once? I doubt Beetle will mind."

"Stop." I feel nauseous. "This is just supposed to be a fun time, Trey. Not serious."

"We'll go out for fast food. How's that for 'not serious'?"

"I'm not sure we should do this."

"Give me a good reason why not."

He folds his arms, and my eyes glaze over his biceps. God, he's stacked. And I know he's only trying to do something nice and genuine for me. I just don't know what to do with that level of kindness.

"I'm waiting, Erin. Give me a reason why we can't do this."

"I…"

I don't have one. Not one that won't break my heart into a million pieces and it's too fragile lately anyway. There are things I haven't told anyone about. Things I don't want to revisit ever again. Things that haunt me every day…

"I don't know why."

Trey nods. "Then we're doing it."

There he goes, once again trying to push me out of my comfort zone. Only I wait for either thrill or dread to hit my gut and neither of those things come. Instead, all I feel is relief. "Okay," I say softly.

"I'm sorry. What was that?" Trey cups his ear, a smile tearing across his handsome face. "Let me hear that again."

"I said *okay*."

"A little louder." He's gloating and looks great doing it, damnit.

"I said, OKAY!"

Trey snatches me by the waist and crushes me against his chest. "That's my girl. Always willing to try new things."

"Ugh. Get off me." I playfully shove away from Trey and manage to push him out of the bathroom with the excuse of having to use the toilet. I hear him chuckling softly in my bedroom while he's, I presume, getting dressed, and I have a full on melt down into my towel.

I don't know what to do.

Staring at my reflection, all I see is a tired, worn-down roadblock.

A selfish one at that.

My mind scrambles to come up with the excuses I'll have to give my son when things don't work out between me and Trey. Because they won't. I know it. He's going places and I'm not.

And I refuse to ever hold Trey back.

Chapter 5

Trey

I'm not sure what the hell happened between Erin and I just now, but until I figure out how to navigate it, I'm going to move slow. I swear she's in the bathroom to avoid me a little longer, and there's a pang of guilt in my belly about it, but I'm not backing down in my pursuit of her until she tells me to.

For now, I'll clean up the mess I made at her dinner table so she doesn't have to.

By the time I hear the toilet flush upstairs — thanks to the old plumbing in this house — I've taken care of everything and just have to wash the dishes. It's not until I hear Erin say, "Oh my god." When I notice she's been crying.

The dish towel in my hand falls to the floor, and I rush over to her. "Hey. Whoa. What's going on with you?"

"I can't believe you cleaned this all up."

Why not? I'm the one that made the damn mess. And the fact that I've taken care of it shouldn't have her voice quivering like it is. I'm on her in an instant, guiding her towards the living room and onto the couch. "Come on, baby. What's wrong?"

"Nothing." She wipes her eyes. "Everything." She sniffles. "Oh my god, I'm a dumpster fire. You should leave. Cut your losses now, Trey."

What the ever-loving fuck is she talking about? "Cut my losses?"

"I'm just going to hold you back. I can't do relationships. I can't even do sex."

It's hard to keep up with her ramblings, but I do my best. "What's all this about?" Because this breakdown isn't because of a fucking dinner date. "And why would you think you're going to hold me back? Hold me back from *what*?"

"From life!" She yells at me. "From success! From everything fun and great and right in your face!"

The only thing right in front of my face is the woman I'm in love with, crying over something I don't understand. I don't want to leave but staying seems to only make her more upset. I just want her happy. "Maybe I should go."

"Maybe you should."

Fuck, my heart falls out of my ass. The way she flips her switch all the time is maddening. Why can't she just give in and let things play out in their own natural way?

Because she's been hurt.

I refuse to be another person in her life that hurts her.

"Okay." I stand to leave, gritting my teeth so I can hold back what I really want to say. I don't get past the coffee table before Erin stands up and grabs my arm. She holds onto me, silently stopping me from going away. God damnit. "I feel like I'm missing some big pieces here. It would be nice to know what they are."

"Look around you, Trey."

I can't seem to break my gaze from her red, puffy eyes. It kills me that she's so upset, and I don't know how to fix it. "What am I supposed to be looking at?" Because I'm pretty sure what I see isn't what she sees.

"I'm a single mom."

I know.

"I'm still in my parent's old house."

I know.

"Look at my sofa."

It's worn down and hideous, but comfortable as a cloud. I don't have to look at it to know it's got stains and a dip on the left cushion because it's her favorite side to sit on.

Erin jabs her finger towards the dining room. "Look at my dinner table. Look at the carpet and the paint and the floor and those kitchen cabinets!"

They could use some TLC. So what? "Are you done?"

"No!" She puts her hands on her hips, and the new pajama set she's wearing looks fantastic on her. Donuts this time, since the penguins are now in the laundry I'd started. "Look at me, Trey."

"I am." My tone is cautious and stern. "I see you with crystal clarity." I drag my gaze up and down her form. Then I nod at the sofa first. "That couch has seen better days. Bet you never wanted to replace it because, one, it was decent when your parents died, and you didn't have the cash to get a new one back then it even if you wanted to. Two, you had a baby, and what's the point of putting new furniture in the house when a toddler is just going to spill things on it. Same for the dinner table, going off the fact that there's marker and paint and glue stuck to it because Beetle went through a big craft phase in kindergarten."

Her cheeks flare red.

I'm not done. "The carpet is stained all to hell because the patio door…" I point to it, "is right there. So Beetle just comes in and out all day long and drags dirt in all the time. *Dirt*," I stress, "from the backyard you've made into a dynamite playground for him." Even though it's dark out, I can see the bike ramp and trampoline in the moonlight. "You're a single mom doing an amazing job with her kid. Just like you were an orphan doing a great job raising her brother."

Erin's shoulders shake as she quietly cries.

"Paint is a pain in the ass to color match," I continue even though it kills me to see her upset, "and I know you're attached to this buttercup yellow."

She sucks in a breath and gawks at me like the knowledge surprises her.

It shouldn't. If I haven't proven that I know everything about Erin by now, then she's not been paying any attention to what I say and do around her.

"How did you—"

I step into her space. "You said, at the graduation party you threw for Glitch, that this was your mom's favorite color and also yours." That was years ago. I remember it like it was yesterday. She wore a light blue sundress and didn't bother to wear shoes the whole time.

Erin drops back down on the couch and covers her face with both hands.

Guess I struck a chord. I'm not sorry about it. "I imagine letting anyone into your extremely fortified and carefully closed off life is hard, Erin." I squat down in front of her. "I'm not here to make it more difficult. I want to make it…" What? Easier? More fun? Anything I say will be used against me or imply that she's not done a banging job by herself. "I just want to be part of it."

"You already are. You have been since *college*."

The way she says "college" clues me in on another underlying issue. One I'll table for now. "I want to be a bigger part of it." That's the bottom line. I can help make things easier and better for her if she'll let me. But most importantly, I just want to experience this life with her. I've spent too many nights imagining being her man and now that I'm so close to having a taste of it, there's no way I'm backing down now.

"I love sharing laughs with you, baby. I love watching Beetle have fun outside. I love the way I walk through your front door and my chest feels light and happy because you're the first face I see."

Even though I know Erin's had a real rough time, she makes life look easy. This woman is an expert at hiding her stress.

Until now, I guess.

Erin swipes her tears and sighs. "I lost my job."

Glitch told me already. "You'll get a new one." If she needs money, I'm sure her brother has it covered. I'll ask him about it later because I'll definitely contribute. "Bet you have ten job interviews lined up for next week."

She chokes on her half-hearted laugh. "Only three."

"Three bomb-ass employers that would be so lucky to hire you."

"They're not what I want, but I'm desperate enough to take whatever I can for now."

I fear she's been doing that since she was eighteen. "What do you *want* to do?"

"Sleep for a week." She knows what I mean, and her snarky answer earns her a pluck on the nose. "Ouch!"

"Try again."

"I want to be an interior designer."

My eyebrows shoot to my hairline.

"Hey, don't judge my skills based on this!" She bristles, waving her hands around. "I've got ideas."

I can't help but look around her living room and try really hard to not offend her with my expression. "Well, you'll give Joanna Gaines a run for her money, I have no doubt."

"You don't think I can?"

It's not hard to imagine Erin barking orders and managing a crew of construction workers, picking out paint and trim, plus arguing with someone about floor installation. I just feel sad that her house is falling to pieces around her—including the hot water heater—and she's not even able to express herself with her own home.

"You're right." Exhaustion laces her tone. "I haven't changed anything here because I couldn't afford it back then, and I don't see the point in it now. My son is a wrecking ball covered in mud most days."

"My mom used to say my brothers and I were hurricanes looking for a place to hit."

"I can't imagine having a house full of boys."

"Mom ran a tight ship. Had to, or we'd plan a mutiny at the first sign of weakness." I sit down next to her. "Money was tight for us all the time too."

My parents worked hard, but bills stacked high because my oldest brother had serious health issues growing up.

"I never meant for any of this to happen." Erin leans back on the couch and stares at the TV that's turned off.

"You mean your parents and Beetle?"

She scrubs her face and sighs. "I mean letting myself get this bitter."

Bitter is the last word I'd use to describe Erin. She's bright, strong, supportive, and under a lot of pressure. But bitter? Never. Sitting down next to her, I put my hand on her thigh. "I'm sorry. I didn't mean to suggest—"

"I know." She smiles at me for a heartbeat. "If I could do it all again, I wouldn't have had my parents die. I mean, their car crash was definitely not my fault. And Beetle..." she trails off for a moment. "I was on the pill and never missed a day taking it, plus we used a condom. Never in a million years would I think with that much protection I'd still get pregnant. But the condom burst, and I guess that one percent was more like one hundred percent that night."

"Damn." I had no idea it went down like that. Glitch never really said much about how Erin got pregnant. He once mentioned that the father had nothing to do with either Erin or her son, so Glitch always took care of things whenever they needed him to, and I never questioned the dynamic. "Have you seen the father at all?"

"I told him I was pregnant the instant I found out."

My entire body coils with her next words.

"He insisted I was lying about him being the father. He threw a wad of money at me, called me a whore, and told me to abort it. He said this baby wasn't holding him back and neither would I. That was our one and only interaction after that night we slept together."

I'm going to find this cocksucker and bury him alive.

"But…" She looks out the window across from us. "I saw him about six months ago. After college, he moved away from here, but I guess he came back to visit family or something. He looked right at me and Brendan as we were coming out of Target. I swear time froze and everything moved in slow motion. He looked me deadass in the face, then at our… *my* son… and kept walking like he didn't see us at all."

Bastard.

"I was so dumbstruck, I almost backed into a light pole leaving the parking lot. I'm not sure what I thought he'd do if he ever saw us but acting like we were invisible wasn't it."

"Would you rather he tried to rekindle a relationship of some kind?"

"God no. He doesn't deserve Brendan in his life." She leans her head on my shoulder and relaxes. "I guess I was hoping that I'd look so spectacular, and Brendan would be so happy and well mannered, that the prick would take one look at what he threw away and then…" she yawns, "lightning would strike him down and he'd blow up or something."

We both start laughing.

"We were always better off without him."

I think she's right about that. Anyone who would throw Erin aside doesn't deserve her. And Brendan? That kid is incredible. He's… everything.

"I heard he's married now, with three kids all under the age of five. I hope they piss in his bed every night."

"Wow! From lightning strikes to bed-wetting."

"I mean, a girl can dream."

Yes, she can. I kiss the top of her head and feel the tension leave her body as she curls up closer to me. "Thanks for cleaning up the dinner mess."

"Thanks for letting me make the dinner mess in the first place."

"I mean, I started it by pouring the wine on myself."

"After I shoved the dishes off the table."

"That was fun and exciting."

"Good." I grab her hand and pull her onto my lap. "I'm hoping for a repeat before I have to leave."

Erin's brow furrows. "How long did you plan to stay in town?"

"I have my laptop with me, so I can work remotely." Am I laying some groundwork here? Yes. "But I do have to get back by Monday for a meeting."

That leaves me with five days to spend as much time with my beautiful girl as possible. Not nearly enough, but it's a start.

Erin looks like she's calculating something. "Do you like your job?"

"Yeah," I say easily. "It's fun. I get to make my own hours and work for some great clients. I mean, sometimes it sucks when I get a pain in the ass client who micromanages, but it beats working in an office nine to five."

Erin lightly chuckles and shakes her head. "No wonder you and Glitch are best friends."

Glitch owns a computer and gaming shop in town. The boy genius got into MIT on a full ride, graduated top of our class, and settled down where his roots were already — back in this small town. He's made a killing with his shop though. The Computer Cave is a haven for kids and there's probably no piece of technology Glitch can't fix. He's worked hard to become successful his own way, and now he's stepping into the next phase of his happiness—marrying the love of his life. I envy him.

When I graduated, I got a job working in the gaming industry. It was fun for about five years, then I took a page from Glitch's book and decided I'd be happier following my passion in graphic design. I'm still in the gaming industry—on the marketing side instead of coding—but I love working with authors most.

After readjusting Erin on my lap, I tuck a few stray strands of her dark hair behind her ear. The sexual tension between us has completely fizzled out, but that's okay. I'm happy to have her in my arms like this.

Honestly, I'm thrilled to have Erin any way I can get her. Naked and on her knees covered in my cum, in the backyard reading a book in her favorite wicker chair, or on the couch in her donut pjs. I just love being near her.

This growing silence between us is getting awkward though. "Want to catch that Scream marathon?"

Erin grins at me. "Yeah. Let's do it." She reaches over and snags the remote from the coffee table and hands it to me. "You find the channel while I'll grab some snacks."

When she returns with a bag of pretzels and two waters, I've got Ghostface on the TV and it's right at the part where the dude sucks the blood off his fingers.

"This is legit my favorite part."

My girl's kinks are wild. I love it.

"Here, get comfy." I wait for her to settle in and then put a blanket on her. She smiles at me, and I swear my heart tries to explode.

I love taking care of this woman, even in small ways like this. Grabbing her ankles, I place her feet on my lap and rub them while we watch the rest of the movie. She falls asleep about ten minutes in. Once I'm sure she's out for the count, I carry her upstairs and put her in bed. Then I crash on the couch imagining how it would feel being married to a woman like Erin and having a son like Beetle.

Hey, a guy can dream too, right?

Chapter 6

Erin

I wake up to the sound of deep laughter. *Oh my god.*

I feel punch drunk as I glance at the clock. It's nearly ten in the morning! Holy shit! I don't know the last time I've slept so late, or so hard. Kicking the sheets off me, I scramble out of bed and rush down the stairs. Glitch and Trey are in the kitchen and the smell of bacon funnels into my nose.

He's cooked breakfast.

He spent the night.

I can't remember anything past sitting down to watch a movie. Having Trey around is bad for my mental health, I'm getting CRS- Can't Remember Shit.

"There she is!" Trey beams a bright smile from the kitchen table.

Glitch sits directly across from him in his usual seat. "Hey. How are you feeling today?"

Like I came too much yesterday and have a lot to do today. "Better."

"Good." My brother takes a sip of his iced tea. "Ara needs some company."

"Huh?" My mouth's too dry. Shit, I didn't even bother brushing my teeth before rushing down here. I'm regretting it now. "What's Ara need company for?"

"I booked her a day of pampering to get ready for the wedding tomorrow."

I drop into a chair and grab a slice of bacon from his plate. Trey immediately shoves an entire dish in front of me. Oh my god. He made me breakfast… and kept it warm under foil. "Wow. Thanks." I peel the tin foil back and see bacon, eggs, and a banana cut up on top of a stack of pancakes. "I love you so fucking much."

He tenses next to me, and I shove a forkful of eggs into my face because I just made a big mistake admitting that. Here's hoping both Glitch and Trey brush it off as a figure of speech. When I look over at Glitch, he's staring at me with a look I'm too confused to figure out. *Focus, Erin!* "What's Ara going to the spa have to do with me?"

"You're going with her."

I gawk at my brother. "No, I'm not. I have too much to get done today. The wedding is tomorrow, this place is a mess, the caterers need to be called and reminded about parking, plus I have laundry to do and groceries to buy." I'm pissed Glitch would even suggest I go with Ara.

Although, I have to admit, the idea of a spa day does sound incredible.

Damnit, now I'm extra mad about it.

I stab into the pancakes and shove a hunk into my mouth. *Thanks a lot for dangling luxury in my face, bro, but I got adulting to do. Like always.*

Trey takes a sip of his coffee. "You still have the gift card I gave you for your birthday last year."

Oh. My. God. Glitch is a rat.

I'm gonna kill him. I'm gonna stab him in the face with my fork for telling Trey I've yet to use his gift card. "I don't have time for spa days." I stab something random on my plate and shove it in my mouth next. Now I feel awful because Trey doesn't deserve my attitude. "It was a lovely gift." I cringe, looking up at him. "I just haven't had a chance to use it yet."

"You do today." Trey's expression reminds me of the one he makes when he watches me suck his cock. "I've already booked services for you. Ara will be picking you up in about an hour, so eat up."

My fork falls out of my hand. "What?" I don't like this. "There's too much to do around here. I can't just—"

"Glitch and I have the wedding preparations handled. It's why I came early and got a hotel."

I feel like I'm floating. "But…"

"No buts." Trey shoves a glass of water towards me. "Eat up and hydrate. I heard that helps before and after ninety-minute hot stone massages."

Ninety minutes? How much did that cost? "Trey."

"*Erin*." He gives me a look that says if I argue with him, there will be consequences.

Joke's on you, fucker. I'm into that shit.

I want to punch him in his mouth and kiss him at the same time. I do neither and end up shoving another piece of bacon in my face instead.

Glitch clears his throat and stares at Trey for what feels like several heart pounding seconds. "We'll take care of the caterers and clean up here, Er. Don't worry about anything."

I want to go, and I can't let myself. "No. I have too much to do around here."

Glitch tilts his head. "Once the services are scheduled, there's a no cancelation policy that goes into effect. You'll have to pay fifty percent of the bill if you cancel less than seventy-two hours out. Is that how you want to spend Trey's birthday gift to you?"

I'm not even sure if what Glitch just said is bullshit or not. "N-no. But—"

"Good, then you're going." Trey tosses his napkin on the table and gets up with his plate.

They're both ganging up on me. I'm not going to win this. And I feel awful that I haven't used the generous gift card Trey got me for my thirtieth birthday. "I don't like this."

"You'll change your mind once you get there." Trey starts washing his dish in the sink. "We've got this covered, mama. Just go and have a girl's day."

Tears spring into my eyes and I shove away from the table before either of them can see how close I am to cracking.

Trey didn't come here to help with wedding preparations. He's come to ruin my carefully constructed fortress and I don't know what to do about it.

Heading upstairs, I take the steps two at a time and slam my bedroom door shut behind me. My hands are shaking. A mix of guilt, excitement, and terror grip me. If I'm going to be honest with myself, I've been dying to use that gift card since the day he put it in my hand. I just haven't had a single free day to use it. And now that I'm unemployed, I didn't feel right using it on myself when money is tight. Yes, I can stay within the budget of the card, and it wouldn't cost me a damn thing, but my brain doesn't work like that. I'd decided to use this gift card once I got a new job.

Which is a lie because I'd be working full-time with no chance of getting a day off to pamper myself because I still have a son to be home for.

That gift card would have expired or gotten lost. There. That's the truth.

A knock on my door makes me jump. *Damnit, Glitch.* "Come in."

Trey pokes his head in.

Rage consumes me and I scream-whisper, "What are you doing up here?"

Glitch will find out about us! If that look he gave Trey downstairs is any indication, he's suspicious already. I'm not prepared for the fallout of something like this yet.

"Relax," Trey says. "He's outside moving the toys and shit out of the backyard."

Guilt bubbles in my belly. "Well, go help him!"

"I will. I just wanted to make sure you were okay first."

"I'm fine," I lie. Skirting past him, I head into the bathroom and start brushing my teeth. Maybe Trey will get the hint and go away.

"You looked like you wanted to claw my face off down there."

I finish brushing and spit into the sink. "The thought crossed my mind."

He leans against the doorjamb and smirks. "All because I'm giving you a day off?"

A day off? That's not what I need. It's not what I want! "You can't just come in here and mess everything up." I rip the hand towel off the hook and wipe my mouth with it.

"What have I messed up?" His tone's changed. I've struck a nerve.

Good. Because he sure as shit stuck a nerve of mine! "You… you can't just take over my life."

"Erin."

"No!" I throw the towel at him. "You can't just stroll in here and act like some kind of hero when you'll just walk back out the next day."

His jaw ticks as he clenches his molars. "I'm helping my best friend prepare for his special day. And I'm just trying to spoil a woman I love while I'm at it."

We both realize what he's said. My heart pounds in my ears. Did he really just say that? I have to grip the sink to support myself. "Get out."

"Erin."

"Get. OUT!"

How dare he drop the L word on me! How dare he have the audacity to look crushed when I turn on him and push him out the door and out of my room. So what if I said it by accident downstairs? That doesn't mean he should say it back!

Slamming the door in his face, I know he sees me breaking down before I can fully shut myself into the bathroom. I'm so damn angry about it I can't wait to get out of here.

I'll go to the spa even if it's just to get away from one thing in my life I can't control.

•••

Trey

I have no clue what just happened, but it's bad. Real bad.

To make sure I don't piss Erin off more than I already have, I head out back and start stacking patio chairs to put them in the shed.

Glitch is pouring gas in the lawn mower. "You want to tell me what the fuck that was about?"

I swallow the lump in my throat. Shit, shit, shit. "Nope."

"My sister's a grown ass woman."

Yup.

"And she's acting like a child."

Pretty much.

"And she only gets this bad when she doesn't have complete control."

I freeze with a massive wicker chair in my hands. Glitch glowers at me, and I swear my balls shrivel. "She's always in control, man. That's never an issue."

"Yeah, well, something's got her confused on that. I think that something is *you*."

Breaking eye contact will give me away and I can't let that happen. "You know how she is better than I do, Glitch. Maybe I overstepped giving her a nice day out with Ara. If that's so, you're just as much at fault as me since this was your idea."

To my relief, Glitch blows out an exasperated breath and shakes his head. "Yeah. You're right. I knew she'd pitch a fit about going, but damn, she never treats herself to anything."

I know. That's going to change.

"You can't just stroll in here and act like some kind of hero when you'll just walk back out the next day."

My stomach twists with her angry words. I'm not the one with relationship issues here, she is. If I have my way, I'll never walk out her front door again. If only she'd stop pushing me away and shutting me out.

And now I feel bad for a million things, half of which I'm not even sure are my fault.

"She needs someone who has the capacity to stop her from being Super Woman all the time."

If Glitch is trying to challenge me, it's working. "Like she'd ever understand it's okay to let someone else take the lead? Please."

Glitch wipes his hands off on his jeans. The distance between us quickly evaporates, as does all the air in the backyard because I'm suddenly face-to-face with my best friend and even though I'm a couple inches taller than him, I feel like an ant.

"Are you?" He growls in his deep voice.

"Am I what?"

"Are you the one who's going to show her it's okay?"

I swallow past the lump expanding in my throat. *He knows*. That's all that's going through my head—Glitch knows about me and Erin and I'm a shit friend for not confronting him sooner with it. I also know how insanely protective he is about his family. Glitch and Erin's parents died before I met them and they're all they have left in the world… besides Beetle and Ara.

And me.

They have me too, damnit.

The realization slides up my spine, reinforcing my backbone. I stare at Glitch and nod. "Yeah, man. I am."

If Glitch doesn't like me being with his sister, now is his time to speak up.

We stare at each other for what feels like an eternity. Sweat's covering our foreheads because it's already hot as Satan's ball sac out here and when we both hear the front door slam shut, Glitch's gaze darts to the fence. We see Ara's car blow by down the road.

His jaw tightens, along with his eyes. "How long?"

Fuuuuck. "Listen, Glitch…"

"How. Long."

"It's… we've been…" Shit. I can't do this. I can't say I've been hooking up with his sister off and on for two years. "Two years."

The tight leash on Glitch's anger nearly snaps. I feel like a piece of shit for keeping this from him, so I confess the rest. "I love her."

That blows him back. So much so, he scrubs his face and stares at the ground for a moment. "You hurt her, and I'll kill you. Best friend or not, Trey, I'll fucking end you."

"I know. But I'd rather die than hurt her, Glitch."

Some of the tension leaves his shoulders. "She's been through a lot."

"I know."

"Yeah… you do." He squeezes my shoulder. "Which is why I'm going to trust you to do right by her… like I have since two years ago when I knew you'd hooked up after the Halloween party."

Okay. My ears and brain must have misfired. "You knew about us?"

"I suspected it. And then every time since, I got more and more suspicious. But this time? She leaves the restaurant, and you chase after her?" Glitch shakes his head. "I drove by her house around two am and saw your car parked out front and the living room light on."

"Stalker much?"

"Had to know if you stayed with her."

"Of course, I did."

Glitch looks up at her bedroom window, his gaze tight and guarded. "Was she even sick?"

"No." Why lie about it now? "She was just… caught up in her head and ran."

Glitch nods, like that's typical of Erin. "She's been judged for most of her life."

I don't say a word, but my hands ball into fists because I'm mad on her behalf.

"She gets happier when you're around, you know." Glitch bumps the side of the lawn mower with his boot. "She doesn't think I notice… but I do."

"She's not happy lately. I can't tell what I'm doing wrong."

"Maybe it's her, not you."

"Maybe it's both." I'm not above admitting when I'm in over my head. "Every time I think I've cracked her shell, she reinforces it tenfold."

Glitch stares at me for several heartbeats. "I don't want to lose my best friend, Trey. If shit goes sideways with the two of you…"

"It won't."

"Sounds like it already has." He points at the open bedroom window, which lets me know he heard us arguing and Erin kicking me out of her bedroom earlier.

"She'll come to her senses." *I hope*.

Glitch laughs shoots a chill down my back. "I hope you have what it takes to pry the reins from her hands, man. Because if you don't, she'll never recover from this."

That makes two of us.

Chapter 7

Erin

After the hot stone massage, that literally made me fall asleep and drool, I met Ara in the tranquility room so we can wait together for our next treatments. "What do you get next?"

"A facial. You?"

"I think a sea salt scrub."

"Ohhhh I have full body wrap experience at the end of the day. I was between that and the salt scrub. Let me know what you think, maybe I'll get that next time."

Next time. Because for Ara, she'll be spoiled—as she should be—by Glitch for the rest of her life. There won't be a next time for me, and honestly, I'm totally okay with that. This place is lovely, but I'm a little out of my element here.

"Sit!" Ara pats the lounge chair next to hers. "Relax and let the aromatherapy soothe your chi."

We both laugh and I lay back, groaning. "I think my bones have turned to rubber."

"Mmm. Heavy rubber."

"Heavy, warm rubber."

We laugh again, and I reach over to squeeze her hand. "I'm so happy for you two. It's going to be fun having a sister."

Ara looks at me, her freshly re-dyed, bright pink and purple hair make her look like a polished gem. "I'm happy to have a sister too. Now how do we get a ring on *your* finger?"

Her question freezes the air in my lungs.

"Come on, Erin. You and Trey aren't fooling anyone."

Oh fuck. "I don't know what you're talking about."

"Mmm hmm." Ara winks at me. "Sure, you don't."

Unable to help it, I crack a smile. I blame the massage, and aromatherapy oils pumping out of the diffusers for my lack of chill.

"Glitch knows," she says. "He confronted Trey already."

My heart lurches up my throat. "*What*?"

"You guys have been hooking up for a couple *years*?"

Oh. My. God.

"Girrrlll, I can't believe you've gone this slow with a guy like that. Trey is…" Ara makes a chef's kiss gesture and I'm reeling. "I'm shocked he's still single, honestly."

My hands curl into fists. I don't want to talk about this. Then again, I *need* to talk about this. Whatever Trey and I have weighs heavily on my chest and only lifts when we're pleasuring each other, and I don't like it. I hate how I feel when he leaves. And I despise being a grown ass woman who's been sneaking around like a teenager. "He's… pretty great."

"Pretty great?" Ara mocks. "No, he's *amazing*. I knew the instant we met that he was one of the good ones."

"Same." And that's the problem. Trey's easy and comfortable and fun and sweet. Why couldn't he be an asshole? "I wish things were different."

"How so?"

"I don't know." Wiggling my toes, I try to pinpoint what the problem is and fail. "He's bossy."

"And?"

"And isn't that enough?"

"Is he bossy or is he encouraging in a take charge way?"

What kind of question is that? "I'm not sure."

"Does it feel good when he's bossy?"

Yes. "I'm not sure."

"Well, you'll figure it out with some more time. For me, I love being submissive. It gives my anxiety and stress a chill out because I don't have to make any decisions. Yet I'm still in charge."

My palms feel sweaty. Is that what I am? A submissive? Look, I'm an avid reader of romance, and I love a dominant alphahole on the page, but Trey's not that. And being in certain situations with him, I don't feel like the one being dominated, even though I guess I am. It just feels different.

Or maybe I have no clue how it's supposed to feel because books aren't always the same as real life.

"He keeps trying to take care of me." I start playing with the tie to my robe.

"Is that okay with you?"

"I love it and hate it. It's nice but feels… off."

"You've been the one in charge for a really long time, Erin. Single moms do not have an easy life. My mom sure didn't while she raised me. Her head never turned off. Her stress never wavered. She was always juggling a million things, plus working her ass off to pay the bills, and still trying to be present in my life, so we had a good relationship. She never had room for being even a little bit selfish. Sometimes I'd try to make her life easier for her and she'd get all upset because even though she appreciated it, she'd say it wasn't my place to care for her. She's the mom, it's her responsibility."

"I feel very seen right now, Ara."

"Well good. Because I do see you, Erin. So does Glitch. And Trey. If he wants to step up and make your life better, let him. See where it goes."

"And if it goes south?"

"Honey, the only thing going south will be his mouth… and his dick."

"Oh my god!" I burst out laughing.

"Where's the lie?"

I can't with her.

A woman stands at the doorway of the room and quietly announces, "Erin, your salt scrub is ready."

That's my cue to get out of here before I start over sharing.

Even if I haven't really said much to Ara, it's feels like a tremendous weight's been lifted off my chest. Glitch knows. Ara's approved. And even though I haven't spoken to Trey since I left the house—and kicked him out of my bedroom—I'm more determined than ever to make up my mind and see how far we can go with each other.

Just as I get to the doorway to leave, I look back and flash an evil grin. "He has a Jacob's ladder."

Ara's eyes widen like saucers. "Holy SHIT!"

Her squeals of excitement make me laugh, and I'm feeling giddier by the second as I leave the room for my next spa treatment. Pulling my phone out of my robe pocket, I send Trey a text message.

Erin: Did he murder you?

Trey's text comes back silently just as I disrobe.

Trey: Not yet.

I guess that's good.

Trey: How is the spa?

Erin: Lovely. Thank you for the gc. I should have used it sooner. My bones are rubber.

Trey: Good to know. I bet you're more bendy now.

Erin: You wish.

"Ma'am?"

I'm startled by the woman waiting patiently for me to disrobe and hop onto the table. "Oh. Sorry!" I shove the phone in my pocket and get ready to be pampered some more.

Only suddenly, I have no interest in staying here for the rest of my "spa experience" and wish I could hurry it all up to get home to Trey. Does that make me desperate?

Maybe I need to take my time here so I can figure out what I'm doing with my life… and with Trey.

Chapter 8

Trey

Erin's alone in the sauna. A little charm and some sleuthing got me this opportunity, and I'm not wasting another second. It's eight o'clock, the spa closes at nine, and Glitch and I made sure to let Ara know she can leave whenever she's ready without worrying about getting Erin home.

So long as I'm around, no one will ever have to worry about taking care of my girl except me.

I've spent the day working my ass off to make Erin's backyard wedding ready while she's been given time to put her feet up for once. It doesn't get any better than that.

Hold up. Yes, it does…

I slip into the sauna and see her leaning back on the top corner of the room, facing the door. I like that she's got her eye on the exit. It doesn't surprise me one bit that she'd be diligent even in a luxury facility.

"How was your day?"

"Exactly what I needed. Thank you."

"I'll have to book you more days like this then."

Erin's deep chuckle makes my dick hard.

It's a million humid degrees in here and I'm still dressed—though I'd gone back to my hotel to shower and change before making my way here, ten seconds in this room and I'm too hot to breathe. "The yard's ready for this weekend."

She doesn't respond.

"The caterer's—"

"What are we doing, Trey?"

I climb the benches until I'm right in front of her. All that's standing between us is her towel and the question hovering, unanswered.

"I've made my intentions clear, Erin." I reach out and run my thumb along her inner thigh as she opens her legs a little for me. "I think the real question is, what do *you* want?" Because she's the queen and ruler of my heart. I won't make a move without her consent.

"I can't tell what I want."

My heart twists from her admission. I know exactly what I want and for Erin to flounder with her desires makes me a little frustrated. But I get it. Change takes time. Letting someone else in takes trust.

I have to earn it.

"I'm scared," she admits.

"New relationships are sometimes scary."

"This isn't new. I think that's why it's scary."

I swallow my rebuttal because she doesn't need promises, she needs action. Talk is cheap. I lean in and press my mouth to hers, fusing us together long enough for me to taste the chocolate she snacked on at some point this evening. "I don't want to be a hero, Erin. And I'm not strolling in and out of your life. I've been a constant for nearly ten years. Ever since Glitch brought me home and introduced me to you and Beetle."

She bites her bottom lip. Skin flushed and sweat dripping down between her breasts, hidden behind her tightly tucked towel, she's like a trapped bird. Will she submit or peck my eyes out?

"I'm not about to walk away from you," I promise. "So long as you want me, I'm yours. I'm here."

I have been since the night we first hooked up. No other will fill the Erin-shaped hole in my heart. I couldn't fuck this woman out of my system even if I tried. She's mine. I'm hers. Now if she'd get on board with this, that would be fantastic.

"I want you to have the life you deserve," I say.

"Maybe I have that already."

"You have a wonderful life that you've worked hard for. Allow me to enhance it."

She snort-laughs. "Enhance." Erin spits the word out like it's a bad joke.

I lean in and try to kiss her again, but she shirks away from me. Damnit. "Why are you *fighting* this?"

"Why are you *pushing* it?"

"Because you're it for me, Erin. If I'm not the one for you, tell me now because I'm starting to feel like a fool."

Her brow digs down. "Do you understand what you're asking for? What you think you want? I have baggage."

"Who doesn't?" I lean in and pinch her chin, forcing her to look at me. "I want your baggage. All your good and your bad. I want to be the keeper of your pain, joy, and tears. I want to be another reason you smile when you come home. I want you to be my pleasure, my purpose. You're my dream, Erin. You're the reason I break every speed limit to get here when I visit. You're the reason I haven't had a Thanksgiving with my family since college. You're the—"

She slams her mouth to mine and shuts me up with a scorching kiss. Her tongue swipes along mine, desperate and hungry.

Now we're talking.

Pushing into her, I all but crawl until I'm between her legs and that fluffy towel is off her body and slung across the bench below us. Her eyes are bright and wild when she looks at me, she's all breathless and worked up. "Please tell me that door is locked."

I flash a toothy grin and nod.

"Thank fuck." She pounces on me, and I grab her thighs, squeezing them while she kisses me again.

Skating my fingers down her damp back, I fan my hands around her plump, round ass and dig in deep enough I hope I leave my fingerprints. Lifting her off my lap, I carefully bring her to the bottom of the sauna where I have easier, safer access to her body. There's a bench in the corner and that's just where I bring her.

Steam billows around us. She smells like lavender and mint. "Did you eat dinner?"

Erin nods. "We ate a couple hours ago at the restaurant on the second floor."

Good. I need her energy up for what I have planned.

"I also had a glass of wine and three waters. The masseuse said I needed to hydrate more... like you said."

I kiss her neck and reach between her legs to see how wet she is already. "Are you still made of rubber?" I test Erin's limits by stretching her leg up over my head. Fuck, she's bendy. Always has been. "Dayem... you're drenched."

"It's the sauna," she teases. "Definitely the sauna."

I love the way she lies.

Erin digs her fresh manicure into my shoulders as I kiss down the valley of her breasts, lick circles around her navel before I sink lower. She's salty and sweet and the only thing I've craved all day. One flick of my tongue on her pussy and I turn feral for her.

"So fucking wet." I make it wetter by spitting on her pretty little cunt.

"Jesus," Erin groans. "How is that so hot?"

I run my finger along her folds, smearing my spit. "Must be the sauna."

"Mmmph." Her eyes roll back when I sink a finger inside her. It takes less than a minute for her to come. Hardly any fun is had before she's shoving away from me. "We can't do this here. It's too hot and I'm…" She swipes a finger between the valley of her breasts that's damp with sweat. "This is going to get gross."

"Hang on." I get up and unlock the door, peering out to see if the large bathroom is still empty. I can't lock the main door, but I can at least get us to a new location. Doubling back, I scoop Erin in my arms and love how she squeaks about it. She's so cute and playful when taken by surprise.

Swinging the door open, steam barrels out with us as I hurry her into one of the massive shower stalls. It's swanky as fuck—rain shower head above us, and two shower heads on either side. A bench wraps around the entire thing and we're right back to where we were, all handsy and starved for each other.

Erin practically climbs me like a tree. I laugh against her lips, feeling alive and thrilled to have her so wound up already.

We both freeze at the sound of the door shutting and flip-flops slapping across the tile floor. Erin looks up at me, her eyes wide and filled with laughter. The stranger starts up another of the large showers, and I get a great idea. "How quiet can you be?"

"As quiet as I want." My girl loves the idea of almost getting caught. "How quiet can *you* be, big guy?"

"Guess we'll find out."

"Take off your pants," she orders while getting on her knees. Damn, does she look good needy. "Now."

"Yes, ma'am." I yank my gym shorts down and pull the hem of my shirt up and over my head. I'm naked in three seconds flat. Erin stares at my cock as I grip the base and pump my hand along its length. "You want a taste of this, my little slut?"

"I've been thinking about it all day."

I lightly slap her in the face with it. Her pupils blow wide, and it makes my balls ache to see it. "Open that pretty mouth so I can feed it to you."

Erin's lips part and she flicks her tongue out to lick my tip. The warm wetness of her tongue elicits a hiss from me. Just the tip. That's all she's sucking on, and I swear it feels so good I could come in no time just from this.

I thread my hand in her hair and shove more of me down her throat. She slides her hands up my thighs, scraping her nails along my skin and my eyes cross. Fuck, she feels good. Even if it hurts, she still feels good on me.

Before I'm lost in sensations that will make me mindless, I gather some strength and refocus. Pumping my hips slowly, I fuck her sweet mouth, carefully reading her cues and behavior. I'm not even a third of the way in and I'm pretty sure I'm almost at her limit.

I said *almost*.

"That's a good little slut." I grip her hair tighter and drive myself inward until I hit the back of her throat. She squeezes her eyes shut, her brow pinched, but she doesn't tap my leg or make a move that says she doesn't want this anymore. I pull out and shove back in, a little faster this time.

Her teeth scrape my shaft.

"Flatten your tongue for me."

Erin's eyes flutter open. They're watery and her lashes are clumped together. It's so pretty. She's a vision with my dick in her mouth.

"Breathe through your nose, pretty whore."

Erin's nostrils flare. Her eyes are deadlocked on mine, her mouth still stuffed with my thick dick. She obeys beautifully.

"That's a good girl." I slide in and out, my thrusts getting sharper each time. Erin digs her nails into my thighs, scraping them hard enough to sting. Then she runs her hands up and around until she has a hold of my ass. She shoves me forward, setting the pace for my thrusts and to my surprise, she shoves more of me down her throat until she's gagging.

Oh it's like that, huh? Okay. Alright.

"You suck me off so well," I say in a low rumble. The shower's still on in the other stall and we're not being as loud as we could be, but we're not being quiet either. "I want to watch you gag on my dick."

Erin sucks in air through her nose and nods with her mouthful. "Mmm hmm."

The vibration of her consent shoots pleasure to my balls.

I grip the sides of her head and start fucking her face. She's so willing to let me, I almost falter. This level of trust only gets my blood pumping hotter. Erin's making all kinds of glorious slurping, choking noises now. Her hands are back on my thighs to keep her balanced while I ram my dick against the back of her throat. Then I hold her like that until she gags, and I feel her throat muscles convulse.

She taps my thigh, and I pull back immediately.

Erin pops off to catch her breath. Drool drips off her chin. Tears roll down her cheeks. She's flushed and red faced and perfect. A woman like this could own the world if she wanted to. She sure as shit owns me as she says, "Again."

"Fuuuuck, woman. You got me too close to the edge as it is."

She swipes her hands through her hair to get it out of her face and stares up at me. "Again, Trey. Please."

Begging for my dick? Yeah, I'm a goner.

I swallow the words I want to say and grip the back of her head as I shove my dick inside her mouth again. "You want this dick so bad? Suck it like it's the only source of air you got."

I kick my hips forward and find a punishing rhythm she can handle. All those lovely slurping, gagging, choking noises return in no time. Erin's willingness to let me use her to get off blows my mind. It's like someone's poured gasoline in my already blazing veins. "You take my cock so fucking well."

She groans against me and starts tugging on my balls.

Hollyyyy ssshhhhiiiiiittttt.

I explode with a climax that has me roaring. Erin chokes and gags, her nails digging into my thighs, but she doesn't tap out. She only holds on for dear life while I empty my load down her throat.

Stumbling back, my dick plops out of her mouth, and I can't catch my breath. Everything's blurry, my heart's racing, and I'm sweating like we're still in the sauna.

Erin swipes her chin, gathering drool and some of the cum that she couldn't swallow because I'd filled her mouth with so much. My knees almost give out when she shoves all four of her fingers between her lips, so she doesn't waste a drop.

"You taste so good, Trey."

I'm speechless. Christ, I feel dizzy and fuzzy-headed and floaty. That doesn't stop me from picking her up, slamming her against the wall and kissing her like my soul's salvation depends upon it.

Erin giggles when she pushes me back a little to catch her own breath. With our foreheads pressed together, she says, "You were supposed to stay quiet."

"Was I?" Oh well. "Maybe she didn't hear me."

"I think the entire state just heard you." Erin doesn't even look upset about it. She leans in and kisses the underside of my jaw, giving me goosebumps. "I like when you unravel from just a little flick of my tongue."

That was hardly a little flick of her tongue. "Well, now it's your turn to get loud."

"I'd rather not hear anymore, thank you very much!" The woman yells out from just outside our stall.

I'm not apologizing for what Erin and I just did. This was too good and fun to regret. "Better leave then," I warn. "I'm not finished having fun with my girl yet."

"Disgusting," the woman huffs, stomping out and slamming the door shut.

Erin frowns, shame colors her cheeks. "She's going to say something to the reception desk."

"So what?" Nuzzling her neck, I take the opportunity to lick a hot trail from her collarbone to her earlobe before growling, "I want everyone to know we're together now."

Erin freezes under me. "About that." Pressing her hands against my shoulders, she shoves me back a little. "I think we need to talk."

Chapter 9

Erin

It's so easy to forget responsibility and adulting when I'm with this guy. All the steam fizzles out of us both once I say, "I think we need to talk." The words came out from fear and panic. Honestly, I'd spent the day enjoying myself with Trey's generosity and even while my feet were being polished and my body wrapped in some kind of lavender I-don't-even-know-what, I weighed all the pros and cons of continuing down Relationship Road with him.

This visit may be for my brother's wedding, but it felt different from the start. I'm not talking about the second our eyes locked at the restaurant last night. I mean… from the *start*.

And dragging him into another fun sexcapade just now feels like a mistake.

I let the day of relaxation, and his ungodly wonderful energy, make me forget my circumstances. That's my fault.

After cutting things short with Trey in the shower, I'd asked him to leave long enough for me to clean up and set my head straight again.

I want everyone to know we're together now.

His words play on repeat in my mind. *Together now?* We aren't together. That implies we're more than fuck buddies.

Because we are.

This isn't just sex. I've fallen for Trey. I don't know when or how, but I have and now here I am, panicking in the women's bathroom about it.

Wow. This rock bottom feels bizarre. I've hit lows before, but this time feels deeper.

Getting dressed, I don't bother blow drying my hair. Swinging the bathroom door open, I see Trey leaning against the far wall, his arms crossed over his chest, his head cast down. He doesn't move until I shut the door quietly behind me.

He looks like how I feel—worried.

I want everyone to know we're together now.

He pushes away from the wall. "Ready?"

"Ummm. Yeah." I tuck my hair behind my ear, my heart banging in my throat.

He opens the door, and we meander our way out to the lobby. I keep my head down, suddenly ashamed of what we did in the bathroom.

"I checked you out already," he says in a low tone.

"I still have to leave a tip."

"Also taken care of."

Tears prick my eyes. He keeps thinking of everything and taking care of it.

I hate it. I love it.

Oh my god, I need to get a fucking grip. Every time I have fun with Trey, it's followed by this unexplainable low that I'm never good at handling. As if he senses I'm floundering, Trey squeezes my hand and I realize how small my palm seems in his.

We stroll past the reception desk and Trey waves at them. "Have a lovely night, ladies." Then he kisses my temple before opening the door for me. The flicker of shame threatening to send me into a spiral dissipates and I'm not sure how that's even possible.

"Come on, sexy mama." He leads me towards the parking lot. "Let's get out of here."

"Wait, I have to let Ara know I'm leaving with you."

"She already knows," Trey says, pulling his key fob out and hitting the unlock button. When he opens the door for me, my stomach flips again.

I want everyone to know we're together now.

I instantly look back at the doors to the spa and bite my lip.

I've spent so much of today imagining a life with Trey—something more than secretly fucking around in a public space. Something where everyone knows that we belong to each other. My heart rate keeps kicking up to stroke levels whenever I think of having something serious with him.

With anyone, really.

I've built walls around myself for so long, I have no clue how to let someone in anymore.

Do I even have time for a relationship, especially considering Trey lives two hours away? Holy shit. It'll never work.

"I think we should keep things like they are now." The words tumble out of my mouth and taste sour.

Trey doesn't respond. Instead, he starts his engine and takes off. I quickly realize we're going in the opposite direction of my house.

"Did you hear me?"

"I always hear you, Erin." His grip tightens on the wheel, and he pulls onto the highway. "Even when you aren't saying things."

I cross my arms over my chest. I've messed this up again, haven't I? Of course, I did. It's what I do.

Something potentially great comes along and I have to smash it before it hurts me.

I don't know how to be in a relationship. I don't know how to let go or give in or work with someone else. I only know how to take care of everything by myself.

We drive in silence for the longest time, and I busy myself by checking messages, texts, and emails on my phone. Beetle usually calls me around nine o'clock to say goodnight and give me a rundown on how his day at camp went. It's eight fifty-five. As if I conjured my son by merely thinking of him too hard, the phone rings and I'm so relieved to see his face pop up on my screen. "Hey!"

"Hi, Mom."

"How was today?"

"Good."

"Yay!" My tone is light and bubbly, like I always make it. "Did you get paired with the counselor you like again?"

"Yup. He showed me how to hold snakes and tell if their venomous or not. *And* we fed a python a rat."

Gross. "Awesome!"

"It was so cool. But kind of sad too because rats are fun. Hey, Mom?"

Oh here we go.

"Can I get a rat?"

"Uhhh."

"What about a snake?"

"Ummm."

"Ball Pythons are pretty small. They only get up to like four feet."

"*Only?*"

"Yeah! And they weigh like five pounds, if that. You can carry it on your shoulders while you garden."

I pinch the bridge of my nose and close my eyes. I love my kid, but no. "How about you start showing me how responsible you can be with your room and chores before we talk about a pet rat or snake or anything else that requires attention?"

"Ugh. I knew you were gonna say that."

I know he's tired of me sounding like a broken record and part of me feels bad that I'm always saying no. Honestly, I'd love to give Brendan anything he wants. But the idea of being responsible for one more living creature isn't something I want right now. And no matter how much he wants a pet, I'll be the one taking care of the damn thing.

"So what did you do today?"

I glance over at Trey before saying, "I actually spent the day at a spa with Aunt Ara."

"Ohhhh."

I chuckle. "Do you even know what a spa is?"

"Not really."

Gotta love this boy. If it doesn't come with fishing line, a remote control, or four wheels and a deck, he's clueless. "It's where you go to get mud masks and your nails done and stuff." Of course, he wouldn't have a clue about places like that. It's not in our budget.

"Why don't you just paint your nails at home like always?"

"Because it's nice to let someone else do it for a change."

Brendan snorts in my ear. "Mom, I love you, but you don't let anyone else do anything for you, ever."

My heart squeezes. "Gee. Thanks."

"I mean, don't be mad at me for it. I'm just saying, you always do everything. I'm really glad you treated yourself. You had a self-care day."

"A self-care day? Who are you and what have you done with my son?"

Beetles laughs at me. "I can't wait to sleep in my own bed tomorrow. Can we have grilled cheese for dinner?"

"Absolutely. Soup too?"

"No. Just ketchup."

Gross. "Okay. I love you, bud."

"Love you too. Bye." He hangs up and I'm dropped back into this surreal space between reality and fantasy, because Trey is definitely a fantasy.

He takes an exit off the highway. "He wants a snake?"

"A ball python. Or a rat." I rub my temples and lean back in my seat.

"Nice. My youngest brother had a ball python once. It escaped its cage, and we couldn't find it for a week."

"Annnd now I'm never getting a snake. Thank you for helping make that decision so easy."

Trey laughs and takes another turn.

Mom, I love you, but you don't let anyone else do anything for you, ever.

Wow. I was just called out by my own kid. I glance over at Trey again and a calmness tries to settle over me. I fight the urge to shake it off. "He…" I bite my tongue. Why should I share a private conversation with Trey? Wait, why do I *want* to?

"He what?" Trey flicks his gaze at me before turning left.

"He said I never let anyone else do anything for me."

Silence envelopes the car.

"He said it like it's a flaw of mine." I sit straighter, feeling myself gear up in defense mode. "I mean, I know he didn't mean it as an insult, but it feels like one."

"The truth sometimes hurts, Erin."

Okay. What the hell? "Excuse me?"

Trey pulls into a parking spot outside his hotel and turns to look at me once he cuts the engine. "Beetle's right. You don't let people help you. It's not a flaw. It's survival."

I'm fucking speechless.

And I'm pissed.

"Take me home."

"Hear me out."

"No. Take me home."

"You wanted to talk, so we're going to have that chat now. Afterwards, if you still want me to take you home, I will. But we're going to talk and we're starting with what you've just brought to me. Brendan didn't say that as an insult, which you just admitted you understood. There's no need to get defensive about this."

"I'm not in survival. I'm just…" Lost, scared, *stuck*. "I'm just busy."

"I know."

"It's not easy being a single mom."

"I know."

"No, you don't!"

Trey straightens in his seat and stares at the dashboard. "Look, Erin, I know what you've been through. I watched you struggle. I watched your brother struggle with you."

I want out of this fucking car. There's no air in here. Scraping at the door, I finally find the latch and yank it, then stumble out. The air is hot and muggy in the parking garage. It's stifling everywhere!

I'm starting to sweat. I can't be here. I can't do this. I'm not good at confronting things like my feelings. It's why I choose to not have any. I'll be happy, sad, or mad for anyone else but myself.

Giving into my feelings hasn't been an option for me since I had to raise Glitch by myself and prove how responsible and mature I was, so the state would never take him from me.

We didn't have any other family. And the distant members have stayed that way—distant. Emotions have no place in my life. Just logic.

So why can't I be logical, damnit?

"Erin." Trey jogs to catch up to me. "Please, stop."

I can't breathe. I can't think. "I'm not in survival mode."

"Okay."

"I can handle everything that comes my way, Trey."

"I know. I've seen it."

"I can raise my kid by myself."

"You have. And you've done an incredible job."

My world tilts on its axis. I can't breathe! "No, I haven't."

"Of course, you have! He's amazing. Beetle's the coolest kid on earth. Smart, funny, easygoing, respectful."

I shake my head. "No. That's not what I mean." I know all of Beetle's attributes and love each one. But… "I haven't raised him by myself, Trey. I did it with Glitch."

And that's how my boy's become the great kid he is. I haven't done it alone.

But I will soon.

I don't think I realized how very important Glitch's presence is, in not only my life, but

Beetle's as well, until lately. Tears sting the backs of my eyes again. I pull at the collar of my shirt, desperate for air. "He's going to start a new life... with his wife. They're going to have kids."

I know they've been trying. Glitch has talked about having his own kids since forever. I can't wait to be an aunt, but where does that put me? Us? Beetle?

I know it's selfish to think like this. But my brother has been all I've had for so long, I can't imagine the dynamic changing. It's been a decade of just us and Beetle. All the grieving over our parents, the fights over dumb shit, the guilt and the resentment–all this time spent doing grown-up things.

I stop dead in my tracks. The world's spinning too fast around me and I cannot get a fucking grip. My heart's going a mile a minute. My cheeks tingle. My chest hurts. I can't feel my legs.

"Hey, whoa." Trey catches me before I realize I'm falling. The garage loses gravity and I'm suddenly in Trey's arms. "Breathe, Erin."

I don't understand what's happening. I haven't felt this way in a long time. "I don't know what I'm doing."

Trey presses our chests together and I all but fold into him like a crumpled flower when he whispers, "I've got you."

I try to follow his lead and remember the steps you're supposed to take when having a panic attack. It feels like it takes forever for me to get in a full breath. It takes twice as long for the blood to stop swishing in my ears. My chest feels like I have razor blades in it. My finger joints ache, and it takes a moment to realize why. I'm gripping Trey's t-shirt so tightly I've stretched it out. "I'm so sorry."

"Nothing to be sorry for."

"I ruined your shirt."

"You didn't ruin anything, and I don't care about my shirt."

"I'm… I just fell apart over nothing."

"It's not nothing, Erin." He pulls back a little and looks down at me. His eyes are soft and lovely. When he sweeps the hair from my face, I feel like he's soothing my soul. That shouldn't be possible. "Can you walk?"

Nodding, I take a step away and lose my balance. Trey catches me before I make a fool out of myself by falling on my ass. "I'm good, just give me a second."

"Let me carry you."

"No." I grab his arm and I'm not sure if I'm pushing him away or using him to remain upright. "I'm just a little dizzy. It's getting better. I can walk."

Really, I want to run far and fast. I'm so embarrassed about my behavior. This is confusing and ridiculous. I can't believe I just cracked wide open in a stupid hotel garage in front of my fuck buddy. I take a few steps again and Trey keeps close with his hand on the small of my back. We enter the lobby and head right for the elevators. I let him take the lead only because I have no clue what floor he's on.

In silence, we rise to the tenth floor, then he escorts me to room 1007. My mouth is dry as he swipes his room card and opens the door for us. The lights turn on and I head straight to the little sitting area. "This is a nice room."

"Got the suite thinking..." He drops his keys and room card on the table. "Well, I just wanted something nice."

Because he thought we'd spend time here together.

"So..." He sits down on the coffee table across from me, resting his elbows on his knees. "Where should we start?"

I'm suddenly too tired to have this talk. "Maybe I should just go."

"No." Trey's tone changes. "If you need a minute to gather your thoughts, that's fine. Shit. Take all night, I have nowhere to be except with you. But we're having this talk before you walk out my door."

He's right. Prolonging it will only make things worse. "I don't think we should be more than we are."

"What are we?"

"Fuck buddies?"

The disappointment in his eyes makes me wish I could take it back.

After gawking at me for a few heartbeats, Trey swipes his mouth with a big hand, and I look at his shiny watch. Then I look around at the hotel room again. Trey likes nice things. Bet his apartment is swanky. His car sure is. And his clothes. He's always so put together. Hell, even when he's dressed in gym shorts and a t-shirt, he's still crisp and high end.

I'm wearing an outfit I bought at a thrift store ages ago, and though I love it, it's getting to the point where there are holes peppering the bottom by the hem. My wardrobe could stand a refresh, but I can't find it in me to splurge on anything new for myself. Whatever money I make goes into the bank for emergencies.

Like being unemployed for the foreseeable future.

Before that, it was video games, sports, and camps.

Before that, it was making sure Beetle had diapers and clothes and toys.

Before that, it was surviving on boxed mac and cheese and hot dogs every night with my brother until he graduated high school.

It's not that I don't have the money, it's that I've been conditioned to never spend it. You never know when your world will turn upside down.

"Why does what Beetle said to you make you mad?"

I stare at Trey, feeling extremely exposed. "I'm not mad."

It's clear by the look in his eyes that doesn't believe me. "You're feeling *something*."

"That's the trouble. I'm feeling."

Trey frowns. "What's wrong with feeling?"

"I tend to not step into feelings. They don't wash out easily."

He nods slowly, letting that sink in, I guess. "And that's your trouble with me too, isn't it? I'm making you feel?"

I look away. I don't even know how to have this conversation. "You probably think I'm a heartless old crone."

His laugh rattles me. "Erin, you're not heartless. And you sure as hell aren't an old crone. Where the fuck do you come up with this stuff?"

"I'm older than you!"

"By three years. Slow down, Mrs. Robinson. Keep that coug'in to a minimum."

My jaw drops. "My coug'in?"

"You don't want to be a cougar?"

"I'm not that fucking old!" I squeal. "Damn, you just cut me deep." I rub my chest like he hurt me.

"MILF then?"

"You're the worst."

"Tell me you know you're a total MILF."

"First, gross. Second…" I fold my arms and shrug sheepishly. "Maybe."

Trey's laughter booms around the room, and it zaps a little life back into me. I smile at him, wondering when this heaviness in my chest will ever ease up and go away. Blowing out a long breath, I turn somber again. "I think Glitch getting married has broken me a little." There. I've confessed it. "Please don't ever tell him that, okay?"

"My lips are sealed." Trey makes an X over his heart. "But why?"

"I've depended on him for a long time. He and Ara are going to have a family of their own eventually, which I'm so excited for, but at the same time…" I trail off, letting reality sink in. "No… that's not what's tearing me up inside." Glitch's happiness will never make me feel the way I do right now. I'm nothing but happy for my brother. Raking my fingers through my hair, I embrace the weight of what's really sitting on my chest. "I'm stuck, Trey."

His voice is soft when he asks, "How so?"

"I never moved out of our parent's house. I let it fall to pieces around me. I've lost my job. Beetle's only at camp because I prepaid for all of it last summer since I could get a discount by paying in full and taking advantage of early registrations for most of them." Now I'm rambling. And avoiding the real truth. "Glitch deserves all the happiness he can get. He had a rough time for so long, and I don't think he'd have made it as far as he has without you."

"He'd have been fine without me. He's a fucking genius and an incredible man."

"You helped him crack out of his shell. He became a completely different person, a happier person once you came into his life."

Trey's face tightens, but he doesn't say a word.

"I had to pick up the pieces and hold us together for a long time. I'm so fucking proud of him and happy for all of Glitch's accomplishments, but..."

"But you're resentful that you didn't get the same opportunities."

My heart cracks in half when I nod. "I was going to go to the New York School of Interior Design. I'd been on a waitlist to get in and two days after our parents died, I got the letter saying I was in."

"Damn, Erin. Glitch never told me that."

"He doesn't know." I've kept a few secrets from my brother over the years, even though I never wanted him to keep any secrets from me. "I knew he'd beat himself up over it, so I tossed the letter in the trash along with my dreams. Then I got pregnant a couple years later, and I never even bothered to…" I cut off from saying anything more because Trey's words from earlier are ringing true. "Oh my god." My voice cracks. "You're right. I have been in survival mode."

I've been in it for so long, it doesn't feel like survival at all. It feels like normal life.

Tears flow down my cheeks. "Why is this hitting me *now*?"

My life has been organized chaos for over a decade. Why am I suddenly realizing it for what it is?

"Change is hard, Erin. And it's scary." He grabs my hands, kissing my knuckles gently. "But all because fear sits on your shoulder doesn't mean you can't still walk the path towards the life you want." He rubs circles on the back of my hands with his thumbs. "Change is scary. Glitch is starting a new part of his life, but that doesn't mean he's leaving you and Beetle behind."

"I know that." I cringe, confessing this next part. "I just wish I was him."

Silence falls between us.

"I want his life." Might as well keep spilling my guts out. "I want to have the courage to step away from my comfort zone and start new things. I want to get out of the house I've lived in my whole life. As much as I love it, I'm attached to it out of fear more than sentimentality. I've grown resentful about so much. And Glitch? Every time he brings up me moving, I get defensive because that's what I do. I argue my reasons for the choices I've made, because getting mad is my go-to reaction." I shake my head and shrink back a little. "I was angry at my parents when they died. How shitty is that? I was so scared and pissed off. Like they died on purpose and flushed my future down the drain." Hugging myself, I look away from him and say, "I'm a shit person."

"No, you're not. You have every right to feel whatever you're feeling. Even if it's misplaced. Grief hits everyone different, Erin. And I don't know anyone else who took on raising a teenager all by themselves and then had a baby and did it all over again from scratch. You're incredible. Seriously, you're the strongest person I know."

"And the loneliest." I lean back on the couch and sigh. "I'll be even lonelier when Glitch and Ara marry and start the next chapter of their life. Maybe I should get that damn snake just so I have company."

"You have Beetle."

"Yeah, until he's a rage-filled teenager who won't even eat dinner with me because he'd rather be in his room with music blaring, playing video games. He's already too cool for me half the time. I have no real friends. Everyone I grew up with moved on and I pushed the rest of them away. Hell, most everyone my age is just now doing what Glitch is — they're getting married, having babies, and likely already have an established career. Me? I'm unemployed and living in a dump."

"Your house is great, don't knock it."

"I don't mean to. I'm just…"

"Needing a change and afraid to make one."

I hate that he's nailed it. "I don't know what I want."

Chapter 10

Trey

Look, I'm not saying I'm a hero, but I know I can make Erin's life better. A woman this spectacular deserves a man who can match her energy and balance her out. She wants a change and is afraid to make any. That'll take time, I suspect, and I'm a very patient man.

I've waited this long already, haven't I?

Since I hooked up with Erin, I haven't been with anyone else. Two years of seeing her only a handful of times hasn't killed me. It makes me long for her more and our reunions that much sweeter. But I'd be a liar to say that I don't want more from her.

I want everything.

But Erin's on edge and I'm going to do my best to get her to relax and enjoy the evening with me instead of worrying about the future. Leaning in, I cup her face. "How can I help?"

She knows what she wants, she's just afraid to take it. Do it. Make it happen.

"Come on, mama. Tell me what you want from me." I want to kiss every inch of her body and I start at her throat. She makes all these little encouraging noises that let me know she'd rather have comfort than a therapy session. I'll indulge for now.

She plucks at the hem of my shirt, lifting it over my head. "I want you to make me feel good, Trey. I want… you."

Erin might be pawing at my body, but I know that's not what she means. I carry Erin to my king-sized bed and crawl on top of her. "Then I'm all yours." Lowering down, I kiss her until she's the very air I breathe.

I'm sure we're going to have more back-and-forth moments, ones where she's floundering and grasping for control, reeling with the need to close up and keep herself safe. But she'll never have to worry about me hurting her. I just need to keep proving that to her.

My lips brush hers. "I've got you."

She's hooking her fingers into the waistband of my shorts, sliding them down my ass.

"Here." I tug her shirt up and help her out of her clothes. We're a tangle of limbs and touches and caresses. Her body is so smooth and soft in all the right places. "I'll never get enough of you."

She flashes me a smile that makes my heart combust.

This woman goes through emotions faster than a tornado can tear up a town. Right now, she's a melting pot of all the lovely things like lust, excitement, and curiosity.

Erin reaches between us and grabs my dick. I take the opportunity to slip her shorts off and toss them to the floor. Laying on her back, her legs spread to give me a spectacular view, she watches me closely. Her look says she hopes I'm happy with what she's got.

I go to the stretch marks on her lower belly, and kiss across them slowly, taking my time to cherish this part of her. Erin quivers a little at first, before melting into my touch. "You're fucking stunning, Erin." Lowering down, I lick and nip at her inner thighs before hooking her legs up around my shoulders and press my mouth to her pussy.

I'm granted with a beautiful little moan.

Before I'm through, I'll have her screaming until her throat is raw.

But I like starting off slow like this. The buildup in my favorite.

"Trey," she groans. "I… I want to rub myself on your dick."

I'll be goddamned. Did she just tell me a desire? I roll her over so she's straddling my pelvis. "Whatever you want, it's yours."

"Good." Erin rubs her swollen pussy along my piercings. "I've been thinking about this all day." She slides against me again, making my toes curl. It feels incredible. It'll feel better when I'm deep-seated inside her.

"That's my girl. Make yourself come and drench me." I grip her hips to help move her faster. "That's right, baby. Take what you need. I want your come dripping off my balls when you're finished."

If we do this much longer, I'm going to come too. Holy fuck, she's slick. I can smell her arousal and it makes my head spin.

"Oh god, oh god, oh god." Her breaths become shallow as her hips thrust faster. She flattens her palms against my chest and uses me however she needs to get off. "I'm gonna come."

She starts making these sweet little noises and moves faster, harder, until I'm pumping my hips to offer maximum friction. Her orgasms rocks the room. Erin tips her head back and screams my name. Before she catches her breath, my girl is already grinding on me again.

"My greedy little slut is already chasing another orgasm, huh?" I reach between us. "Lift up."

She does what I want, and I run the head of my dick in fast, short strokes against her clit. The friction feels good, even to me. My balls tighten as Erin comes again. She drapes her body against mine to catch her breath for a minute.

"Condom," she rasps. "Get a fucking condom on, please."

Since she used her manners…

I reach blindly for the box on the bedside table and manage to fish one out. Tearing the wrapper with my teeth, she backs off me and watches as I slide it over my length. I'm careful about it, especially with my piercings.

Before she can climb onto me again, I turn her over and take charge. I'm a big guy. Erin might be worked up, but she's going to need more foreplay before I can fuck her. Licking her clit, I work one, then two, then three fingers into her pussy. She's so swollen and slick, I'm faltering just listening to the wet noises her body makes for me.

"Ready?" I kiss her deeply as I push my head against her pussy. I barely get it in before I start sucking on her tongue to help distract her. One thing I've learned with Erin is: She likes being overwhelmed even if she doesn't realize it. My girl lives for organized chaos.

So I'm going to give it to her.

Collaring her throat, I suck on her tongue a little longer and shove in another inch. Then I kiss her deeply and push in a little more, being mindful of how she reacts as I fill her.

"Tell me if it hurts."

She nods before tipping her head back. By the time I'm halfway in, she's making little noises and clutching my shoulders. "Holy shit, Trey."

I nip her neck and work my way to her shoulder while she continues to take inch after inch of me. "How's that feel?"

"Huge."

I laugh. "I mean the ladder."

"*Amazing.*"

I wasn't sure how the piercings would go with a condom, but there was no reason to think she couldn't enjoy them, even with a small barrier between the two of us. I'm glad it pleases her so much. Looking down, I watch my dick slide in and out of her. My shaft glistens with her arousal. Her pussy is wrapped around my cock so tightly, and the view is so damn spectacular, I shove more of myself inside her.

She sucks in a harsh breath.

I pull out slowly, loving how her pussy grips me so tight. "Take all of me, Erin." I want to drive into her, but I don't want to hurt her.

She lifts her head, her eyelids heavy and sultry as she smiles. "I want it all, Trey. Everything you have, I want it."

I shove forward and bottom out.

• • •

Erin

Big, big, big-big-big!

Trey's intimidating in his gym shorts but having his monster cock inside me is next level fantasy smut. Don't get me going on the piercings. Holy shit, if anyone ever gets a chance to fuck a man with a Jacob's ladder, do it. Live with no regrets.

I'm still trying to adjust to his size when Trey pulls out and shoves back into me. I have no idea how I'm able to take a big dick like this, but my body welcomes every inch, and I love the painful pleasure he brings. I'm already buzzing in my head. I feel so full, so stretched, so...

"You're doing so well," Trey growls, staring down at our joining. "Fuck, Erin, your cunt is so pretty wrapped around my cock like this."

I squeeze my inner walls in response, and his eyes blow wide. "Fuuuuck. Don't do that again until I say."

I do it again anyway.

"SHHHIIIITTTT." His hips jack forward, and his pace quickens. "God damn, I've wanted this for so long, I'm not gonna last."

I've come twice already, so as far as I'm concerned, he can chase his release now, or fuck me into the dawn. I'm just happy we're doing it and my thoughts have turned off.

His abs flex with each thrust. Sweat glistens across his brow. His fingers dig into my thighs and I'm sure he'll leave bruises. Lifting my hips, I beg, "Harder."

My cue catches him off guard. "I don't want to hurt you."

"You won't."

He pauses long enough for the meaning of our words to register. He exhales slowly before leaning to kiss me, "No, I won't hurt you. Ever."

I'm going to let go.

I'm going to try and have a relationship with Trey.

I'm going to let myself love him in every way.

"Harder." But right now, I need to be blown apart. "Give it to me, Trey."

"Fuck, woman. You're treading in dangerous waters here."

I bet. He's big and wound up and has a lot more talent in the bedroom than me. I want to experience as much as I can tonight. "What have you always wanted to do with me?" My breath flies out of my lungs when he slams home. Holy shit, he's going to rearrange my guts.

Trey doesn't speak for a moment, he just rams into me over and over, driving us up the bed until my head smacks the headboard.

"There aren't enough condoms in that box or hours in this night to do everything I want with you." He keeps driving into me and I'm starting to feel that familiar tightness in my belly. If he gives me an orgasm by just fucking me, that'll be a first for me.

I usually need a lot of friction on my clit to get anywhere near an orgasm.

But he keeps hitting something inside that feels phenomenal, and I'm barely able to enjoy because he's already pulling out. "Trey, no!"

He grabs my hips and flips me over. "Ass up, slut."

My face is buried in a pillow when I tip my butt in the air. *Thwack*! He spanks me just hard enough to make my pussy clench. "Oh my god." I clutch the sheets. *Thwack*! He spanks me again.

"You gonna let me take care of you, Erin?"

I lift my head, confused. "What?"

Thwack! He does it again. A delicious burn spreads across my ass and my eyes roll in the back of my head when he shoves his dick back into me.

"Answer me. Are you going to let me take care of you?"

My entire body rocks against his while he fucks me harder. "Y-y-yes."

Thwack! "I can't hear you."

"YES!"

"That's my good little whore." He drives into me, hitting a deeper spot in my body that dances along the edge of pain. I love it. I had no idea I needed it until…

"I'm gonna come again." My lungs hurt to draw in air. My hair sticks to my sweaty forehead and back. "Please, don't stop."

"My greedy girl thinks she can come a third time?"

"P-please." Holy shit, my world is being R-O-C-K-E-D.

"Since you used your manners…" Trey spreads my ass cheeks and I think he spits on my tight hole. I'm too far gone in a delicious headspace to fully comprehend what's going on. But when he fills my ass with something—*his thumb maybe?*—and continues to fuck my cunt, I fly apart.

"That's it, Erin. Let go." He drives into me over and over and over and—

"TREY!" My body locks as my climax roundhouse kicks me off a cliff.

"Awww yeah." He holds me close as I spiral. "That's it, baby. Come all over my fucking dick." He pulses inside me. I swear he grows bigger. "Your pussy grip is next level, woman. Holy fuuuuck."

I can't even respond. My body's on fire and I'm boneless and floating. My inner walls just keep clenching and pulsing and when Trey finally withdraws I slump, face-down onto the mattress.

His weight envelopes me, pressing against my back as he kisses up my spine and the back of my shoulder. "You okay?"

"Mmmph." I wish I could say more, but I can't make my body or mouth move.

The mattress shifts as he leaves the bed. I assume he's throwing out the condom and getting dressed. My eyelids are too heavy to keep open. I barely feel something warm swipe between my legs. I can't even care that he's lifting me and moving me around like a rag doll.

I let myself go tonight, which felt incredible.

But what will the fallout be in the morning?

Chapter 11

Trey

I look up from the couch to check on Erin. She's still sleeping. I'd love to take credit for knocking her out last night, fucking her so good she passed the fuck out, but I'm man enough to also admit she's probably just exhausted and catching up on some Zzzs. I take advantage of the morning by ordering room service and getting a bunch of remote work finished.

Checking my emails, I confirm my appointments for later this week and scroll through social media and real estate sites. I'm just about to take another sip of coffee when a gasp breaks my focus.

Erin shoots up from her pillow, her bedhead all kinds of whacked. Her eyes dart around like she can't tell where she is.

Setting my laptop and coffee down, I saunter over to her. "Morning, sleepyhead."

"Holy shit." She rubs her eyes, smudging her leftover mascara more. "What time is it?"

"Ten thirty."

"Oh my god!" She scrambles out of bed like her hair is on fire and her legs get tangled in the sheets. She starts kicking them off like a mule, which doesn't do anything but give me a great view of all I had to play with last night. She manages to free herself and almost falls out of the bed, because she's in such a hurry.

"Whoa now. Where's the fire?"

"Beetle's going to be home by noon! I have to go!" She starts gathering her clothes, wincing as she bends down to snag her shorts.

"Sit down and have breakfast first."

"Trey, I can't! I don't have time."

"Yes, you can and yes, you do. Now sit." My voice might be stern, but my expression remains warm as we have a stare down. "There's plenty of time, little mama. And these blintzes aren't going to eat themselves."

She's arguing in her head about whether she should obey or bolt. I can tell by the way her lips purse.

"I promise I'll have you home with plenty of time to get Brendan off the bus."

That settles her nerves enough for her to sit on the edge of the bed. Sauntering over to the room service cart, I lift the lid on the plates and am disappointed that all the food's cooled to room temperature. Not that I would have awakened her for a hot breakfast, but damn.

"I haven't slept that late in… well, since yesterday. But before that I haven't slept past six am in forever."

Both days she's slept in and gotten a decent amount of rest are the same two nights I've stayed with her. Does she realize that?

I carve into a blintz and stab a strawberry with it. "Here." Feeding her like this is nice. I could get use to this.

"Did you eat already?" She licks a little cheese off the corner of her mouth.

"No, I waited for you. Got some work done, so I should be free for the rest of the day."

"Efficient early bird, huh?"

I don't say that I barely slept last night because I stayed up watching her instead. She snores like a little puppy and kicks a lot. Twitches too. I also don't tell Erin that I held her for hours, imagining doing it every night for the rest of my life.

She eats her breakfast in bed with her legs crossed and mascara smeared on her gorgeous face. My beautiful, chaotic mess. I'd sell my soul to wake up to her every morning with breakfast.

We eat in comfortable silence. There are a million things I want to say, but now isn't the time. She keeps watching the clock, and it makes me anxious. "I promise I'll get you home before he's there, okay?"

She nods but doesn't look convinced. Scarfing down her food, I fight the urge to tell her to slow down. She's probably eaten fast her whole life, always in a hurry to get to the next thing on her ever-growing to do list. But barking orders at her constantly will make me seem bossy, and I don't want to turn her off.

I really wish she'd slow down a second, though.

"Can I take a shower here?"

"Of course." She doesn't have to ask me something like that. Whatever she wants, she's going to have when I'm around. "Come on."

"I don't want to waste the opportunity to have a long, hot shower," she explains.

I hate that she's been taking cold ones for so long. Bet Glitch has no idea her hot water heater's busted, because I know damn well he'd have it replaced, with or without her approval. I'd do it myself if I didn't fear she'd accuse me of overstepping.

When I see her wince again, guilt stirs in my belly. "Are you sore?"

"A little. But it's a nice ache."

I hate that I might have hurt her last night. "I'm so sorry. I'll be more gentle next time."

"If I want gentle, I'll tell you. Don't you dare hold back on me otherwise, Trey."

I smile and nod. "Yes, ma'am."

Look, like I've said before, I'm a big man and a lot of women do not want someone my size. It's not just intimidating, it's painful. But last night Erin took every inch like her body was built for me to fuck and I'm going to take every opportunity that arises to make her scream my name and come.

Starting the shower, it's hot in a matter of seconds.

"Those should be illegal." Erin frowns at my white gym shorts.

"Why's that?" I know why. But I want to hear her say it.

"I can see the ridge of your dick through those flimsy things!" She runs her fingers along my shaft, groping me through the thin fabric.

"Careful, mama. Don't start something you can't finish."

"Who said I can't finish?" She squeezes my dick and arches her brow at me.

Fuuuck this woman is going to break me. She drops to her knees and tugs my shorts down.

My dick hardens in her hands while she licks the head and plays with my piercings. "Why'd you get these?"

"Why not?" I suck in a harsh breath when she grazes her teeth along my length. Goosebumps erupt down my arms and thighs.

"They look and feel amazing."

"*You* look and feel amazing," I growl back when she drags her tongue across each piercing before sucking on the tip again. "Goddamn, Erin, you're playing with fire."

"Burn, baby, burn." She grips my balls and pulls them down while taking as much of me into her mouth as she can.

Threading my hand in her hair, I rock my hips slowly and hold the base of my dick with my free hand, feeding it to her. "Greedy girl. You suck my dick so fucking good."

Erin's eyes flutter as she looks up at me.

I pull out and back away. "Get in the shower."

She looks caught off guard. "What? Why? Did I just do something wrong?"

"Not at all," I say, already heading back out to the bedroom. "I'm just trying to stay on track and you on your knees derails me." I rush over to grab a couple condoms then come back.

She's just wetting her hair when I step in to join her. "You are the prettiest woman in the whole wide world, you know that?"

Erin chuckles. "Yeah, my saggy ass brings all the boys to the yard."

The way she belittles herself pisses me off. I reel back and crack her ass with a fast strike.

"Hey!"

"Talk like that again, I'll punish you again."

Her green eyes are bright and fiery as she stares me down. Without saying another word, she grabs the little hotel bottle of shampoo and dumps some into her palm. She washes her hair and I take the moment to appreciate the view.

Erin's hips flare out in a beautiful spread. Her tits jiggle when she moves. I love that she's painted her toes a deep blue almost as much as I love that her fingernails are glossy black. She tips her head to rinse out her hair and I bend down to suckle on one of her big nipples.

She falters a little, but I hold her close to me. "Are you too sore to take me again?"

Her answer is soft and quiet. "No."

I've had a condom in my hand this whole time, hidden from her sight. Ripping it open, I get it on while she watches me. When our eyes lock, my heart skips.

"If it's too much, tell me to stop." I reposition myself, crouching down for the best angle, and lift her leg to hook around my waist. Rubbing the head of my dick against her clit, I build up her arousal and have her panting in no time. "That's a good girl." I shove into her a little and she doesn't protest. Reading all her cues, I slowly make my way inside her until I'm nearly buried balls-deep. I keep moving instead of giving her time to adjust.

She seems to love it.

Grabbing Erin's ass, I lift her up and press her back against the wall. Hot water pummels us. Steam billows. My heart pounds as I hold her close to me and fuck her slowly.

"Use me," she begs. "Use my body to get off."

"I'm not using you for anything, Erin. We come together or not at all."

"I don't want to come. I want you to use me," she says again, her breath hitching when I hit a deep spot inside her.

I still, worried I've hurt her again. "You okay?"

"Oh my God, put me down."

The mood flips that fast, and I pull out and set her on her feet. She steps out of the shower and grabs a towel, leaving me confused and pissed off.

"The fuck, Erin?" Because I've done nothing but be a gentleman this morning, so what's her problem? Turning the water off, I step out and glare at her. "Talk to me!"

"You said to tell you what I want. I want you to use me! That's what I want." She throws her towel at me. "I want you to pretend I'm so sexy you can't even control yourself around me. I want you to use my body to get off on like I used yours last night."

Oh, so it's like that, huh?

I saunter over, my hard dick bobbing like a heavy weight between my legs. "I don't have to fucking pretend, Erin. I never have with you." To make it clear, I spin her around and bend her over the vanity. Kicking her legs out, I run my hands down her backside and slap it not once, but twice. "Now take my cock like a good fucking whore and make me come."

I shove into her with enough force to knock the breath from her lungs. Erin knows how to tell me to stop, so when she cries out my name instead, I keep going. I use her. I fuck her like she's the object of all my desires. I thrust into her body like she's my only salvation and I've sinned for far too long. I grab her hips to keep her aligned and rail her over the sink until my balls draw tight.

Her hands flatten out against the mirror in front of us to hold steady. "Holy shit."

"Look at us," I growl, forcing her to watch our reflection. "Look at the animal I become around you."

Our skin slaps echo in the bathroom.

Erin can't catch her breath and I don't even want her to. Collaring her throat, I tip her back and keep my thrusts steady as I hold her against my chest. Her mouth's open as she pants. I reach forward with my free hand and rub her clit while I slam into her, swirling my hips with every other thrust.

"Shit, shit, shit, oh my god!" Erin's voice rises with my heart rate.

My climax barrels down, making my spine heat and sweat bloom down my back. "Gonna fill you up. And you're gonna take every drop, aren't you?"

"Y-y-yes."

She claws at the vanity, and I let go of her throat to slap her ass again. "This is mine. Understand?"

"Yes."

I pinch her swollen nub and growl, "No one better touch this sweet pussy but me, understand?"

"Yes." She rises on her tippy toes, still taking my pounding like a good girl.

"These tits are mine." I grab them both and squeeze until she cries out. "Understand?"

"Y-yes. Holy shit, yes, don't stop. Don't stop!"

"You don't get to call the shots, slut. You're mine to fuck. Mine to come inside. Mine to play with." I wind her hair around my hand and pull it. "Do you have any idea what you do to me? How much you drive me fucking crazy?"

"N-n-no." She can barely speak. Her entire body rocks from my thrusts and she's turning flush.

"No?" I spank her again. "I think that's a lie. I think you know *exactly* what you do to me. You wore that dress the other night knowing it would drive me wild. All that leg showing. And your tits spilling out of the top. The curves you showed off for everyone to see."

She starts making all these little whimpers and squeaks.

"I should have fucked you in that restroom. Made everyone there hear you scream my name." I slam into her over and over, my balls drawing up tight with my impending release. "I can't stop thinking about you. Ever." *Slam, slam, slam.* "And last night, while you slept, I wanted to jack off all over you and fuck you awake and stuff my dick in your mouth, your cunt, and your glorious ass."

Erin's pants become ragged.

"But I let you sleep instead. And now look at me. You've turned me into a rutting beast. So desperate to come inside this pussy that belongs to *me*." I shove Erin down so her chest smashes flat against the counter. "Fuck, you feel so good."

Erin's inner walls squeeze, and that grip of hers sets me off. I come so hard I see stars. Keeping us locked together, my fingers dig into her hips as my cock throbs, my load spilling out of my body with strong pulses.

My heart jackhammers in my chest. My lungs burn. Carefully, I pull out and run my hands down her back. "Are you okay?" I toss the condom in the trash while keeping one arm hooked around my girl to hold her up. "Talk to me, Erin."

"I'm… yeah… I'm okay."

She's scissoring her legs together, and her eyes are tightly closed.

"What's this?" I tease, pressing the heel of my palm against her clit. She lets out a groan and pushes into me, seeking friction. "I thought you didn't want to come."

"I might have changed my mind."

Good. Because I had no plans in letting her leave without coming on my face at least two more times.

"Whose pussy is this, Erin?" I gently pull her hands back so she can't touch herself.

"Yours."

"That's right. And I take care of what's mine."

I drop to my knees and fuse my mouth to her cunt. Locking onto her clit, I suck it in short bursts.

"Yes," she grunts. "Please, don't stop."

Never. I will die on my knees for her.

Running my hands all over her body, I grab, twist, pull and caress a little bit of everything. She shudders with her orgasm, rocking into my face until she's ridden it out. "Holy shit," she whispers, still trying to catch her breath.

I stand up and capture her face with both hands, pressing my head to hers. "You're incredible."

Her laugh bubbles out of her. "I didn't even do anything. You did all the work."

Fucking her will never be work but I get what she's saying. "You did more than you think. Was it…"

"That's just what I wanted." Erin sighs and I love how her cheeks are all rosy. "I loved it."

I don't want her to ever feel used. I already call her a slut and a whore because she asked me to a while back. But I also know that she wants to feel cherished and lusted for. I thought I'd been doing a good job of that all along, but maybe she wants it expressed this way too.

I can work with that.

• • •

We pull up to Erin's house by eleven-thirty. She's sore, that much I can tell with how she sat gingerly in the car. But she's also on cloud nine, going by the serene, freshly fucked look on her face.

My pride swells knowing I had something to do with her current state of mind.

We enter the house, and my chest warms with the smells of this place. I'm not ready to scare her by saying it smells like home to me, but it does.

Erin immediately starts checking out the work Glitch and I did in the backyard. "Wow." She steps out onto her back patio. "This looks like a whole different property."

All we did was clean up the toys and bike ramps and collapsed the trampoline. Mowed and moved furniture around. The caterers came in to set up the rollout fabric that covers the mini dirt track and set folding chairs up.

"That arch is perfect," I say, placing my hand on the small of her back.

She leans into me and sighs. "My dad built it for my mom. She had twinkle lights on it over there," she points at a different part of the yard. "But I moved it here and planted Clemantis on it. It'll look even cooler when they're in full bloom."

"Stunning," I'm not talking about the flower. "What's over there?"

"Roses and wisteria. Over there are day lilies. The tulips are done, but my Lucifer plants are popping up. They've done well out here."

My gorgeous girl loves to garden, and her landscaping is phenomenal. "It's amazing." *Like you.* "Smells good too." *Like you.*

She looks up at me with a content smile. "Gardening's my happy place."

And you're mine.

The sound of a deep engine rumbles to a slow stop. Erin immediately shoves away from me. "Beetle's home!" She runs into the house and stands in the front doorway to greet him.

I come up right behind her, and watch Brendan hop off the bus. He hoists a book bag nearly as big as he is onto his shoulder and his brow digs down while he walks along the sidewalk. Then he sees my car in the driveway. My heart clatters because I'm not sure what I should expect, but it's not the reaction Beetle gives.

A smile tears across his face as he runs across the lawn. "Is Trey here?"

Damn does my heart swell hearing the excitement in his voice.

"Yes!" Erin laughs, like his enthusiasm about me visiting is totally normal.

Beetle breezes into the house and shoves right past his mother to see me. Happiness lights his face when he drops his bag and yells, "TREY!"

"What's up, little man?" We do our secret handshake that I taught him last time I came to visit. I catch the look on Erin's face—it's warm and loving and it tears me up inside.

Our eyes meet, and she shakes off the emotion and puts her hands on her hips. "Hey!" Erin fusses. "What am I? Chopped liver? Seriously, kid, I give you life, and you just blow right past me to go to the cool guy first?"

Beetle rolls his eyes, which is a total contradiction to the big smile still plastered on his face. He spins around and dives into her with a hug hard enough to make her stumble back. "Ohhhh, I've missed you." She kisses the top of his head and pulls back with her face scrunched up. "Holy crap. Did you shower at all this week?"

"No way. I'm not using those showers."

"Oh my god, Brendan." Erin points at the steps. "You're still in the same clothes you left our house in a week ago!"

"At least you won't have to do extra laundry."

She groans into her hands. "Go de-funk yourself in the shower."

"I don't smell that bad!" He sniffs his shirt and frowns. "Okay, well now that I'm home, I might stink a little. But at camp we all smelled the same. No one showered."

"Ewww!" Erin shivers. "Go get cleaned up and I'll have lunch ready when you're done."

"Grilled cheese, right?"

"Yup. Nothing but the best for you." She winks at me before saying, "And guess what Trey brought?"

"The new Screaming Falls video game?"

"Uhhhh…. I was going to say guacamole and chips from the Salty Cantina."

I laugh and correct her. "I brought both, little man."

Beetle's eyes grow the size of saucers, and he fists bumps the air. "Yes!"

"Better listen to your mama if you want either one, though."

Beetle races up the steps and heads straight into the bathroom.

Erin sighs, and our gazes meet again. To see the joy on her face having him home warms my heart. "He really loves you." And why not, Erin's an incredible mother.

"He also really loves you," she says cautiously. "We need to be careful, Trey."

I hear what she's not saying: If it doesn't work out between us, our hearts won't be the only ones to break.

Chapter 12

Erin

"You may now kiss the bride."

I juggle my bouquet, and Ara's, so I can clap with the rest of the guests. Tears fill my eyes, and I'd love to blame it on sun glare, but what would be the point? Glitch, escorts his new bride down the makeshift aisle in my backyard and I follow behind, hooking my arm with Trey, the best man.

He flashes me a smile that makes my heart skitter around and I work hard to keep my gaze forward until we make it inside the house where I slip my arm out of his. "This is a happy day."

"Definitely. I haven't seen Glitch smile this much in…"

"Ever," I finish for him. I've never seen my brother this happy in his entire life. My heart squeezes with both joy and envy. I want happiness like this too.

As we each grab a flute of champagne, I reset my emotions. The back patio doors are wide open, making my house feel like its guts are spilling into the backyard.

"Pictures!" the photographer, Carson, announces. "I need the bridal party over by the archway."

"Aw, come on, man." Glitch wraps his arms around Ara. "Put your camera down for a minute and enjoy yourself."

"It'll only take a minute."

"It better," Glitch says, nipping Ara's fat bottom lip. "I've got plans for us and don't want to wait anymore."

Ara smacks his arm. "Pictures are important!"

"So is making you purr, *Kitty*."

Oh for the love of all things unholy. My ears will never unhear that.

I clap my hands and start hauling ass to the arch covered in my deep purple flowers, if only to get out there before my eyes bleed next. I do *not* want to see my brother groping my new sister-in-law, fuck you very much. "Picture time!"

At least the wedding party and guest list is small. And the photographer, who's a friend of Glitch and Trey's, seems super nice. "Where do you want us to stand, Carson?"

Beetle joins me, yanking on his bowtie. "This thing is too tight. I hate tuxedos."

"You look good though, little man. Sharp."

Instead of bitching about wanting to change into a t-shirt and shorts like I expect, Beetle rolls his shoulders back and seems to grow confidence right before my eyes.

I fight the urge to glance at Trey. He's good for my son.

I think he's good for me too.

I don't know how to feel about it.

"Stand next to your mom," Carson orders. "Trey, get in close."

Why is he taking pics of just us? "Wait, what about Glitch and Ara?"

"They snuck off already."

You've got to be kidding me.

"It's okay, I want to get some shots of you guys and I'll take care of the rest when they come back." Carson starts snapping pics and each time he puts us in a new pose, my heart clanks louder against my sternum.

Carson tips his chin at my son. "Go grab your bike."

"It's packed away," I say with a frown. And what's he want Beetle's bike for? It's not like he can ride in the backyard at the moment.

"It's in the shed, I'll have to grab it." Trey heads over to the small building that holds most of my storage and all my garden tools. "We had to play Tetris in here with all the Halloween decorations to make the yard stuff fit."

"You like Halloween, huh?" Carson snaps another random picture.

"It's the only holiday I actually love." Spooky season should last all year round if you ask me. "Why do you want Brendan on his bike?"

"Glitch said he's good at trick shots. Figured I can capture some of it for you while I'm here. It'll look fire with him in a tux. Hey!" Carson yells at Trey. "Grab his skateboard, too, if you can."

"He'll get all dirty!" I don't know why I'm arguing. I want these pics, to be honest, but I also feel lost right now and out of control in my own house.

"We're all going to be ruining our clothes as soon as the newlyweds show back up, Erin." Trey carries over my son's BMX bike that used to belong to Glitch, as well as his freestyle skateboard. "Or did you forget?"

How can I possibly forget Ara wants a paint battle in the front yard where we're all going to wreck the dress and shoot each other with paint-filled water guns Glitch rigged up?

This is, by far, the whackiest wedding ever.

"Okay, my dude, let's take this stuff out front and make some magic happen." Carson lures Beetle off and I'm stuck standing under the arch with no clue what to do.

The caterers are handling everything — including breaking down the seats and aisle and moving in the dining tables and centerpieces. The yard is bustling around me, my house is filled with strangers enjoying appetizers and cocktails, and my son is riding his bike in a tux.

It's a fucking circus and I'm not even the ringleader at this point.

"You look stunning." Trey knocks me out of my frazzled thoughts by kissing me.

I feel like everyone's staring at us. I feel guilty and I can't figure out why. I catch myself trying to duck away.

"We don't have to hide anymore, Erin."

All because my brother knows about us doesn't mean we shouldn't be cautious. My son doesn't have a clue that we're.... together.

Trey ran his hand down my thigh under the table yesterday while the three of us ate lunch and I nearly leapt out of my seat. He must have sensed it too, because he squeezed my leg twice, as if telling me to calm down and behave myself. He didn't let go of me, even after Beetle ran into the living room to play video games for a little while.

And now he's kissed me in front of everyone.

I hate feeling confused about it.

"Smoke's going to start funneling out of your ears, little mama." He boops the tip of my nose and walks off, his hands in his pockets as he makes his way back into the house.

God, his ass is fine.

Trey's tall, built, and swaggers without showing off. His confidence is almost calming.

I don't know why I keep letting myself second-guess things with him. I need to stop.

I need to chill.

I need to...

"Hey, Mom! Check out what Carson caught me doing!"

Jesus Christ, how long have I been standing here stuck in my head?! I blink a few times, resetting myself—again—and smile at Brendan. "Let me see!"

Carson pulls up the photos on his camera screen and starts clicking through them. "He's a natural."

"Wow." I can't believe these pics are even real. "These are amazing." Brendan's in his element and reminds me so much of Glitch when he was that age.

"Done already?" Trey comes back to join us, and I swear his timing is too perfect. What was he doing, watching me from inside my living room? He takes the camera and starts clicking through the shots. "Amazing."

"Of course, it is. I'm the best of the best." Carson snags his camera away. "And don't touch my baby. She doesn't like being manhandled by anyone but me."

The two of them laugh and Trey's eyes fall on me. "I know all about that."

• • •

I have to admit, that paint gun battle was a blast. I'm covered in head-to-toe washable colors and feel like a bag of Skittles left out in the rain, which is way more exhilarating that I would have guessed.

The stairs creak like always and I hold on to the banister with one hand, lifting my dress with the other, as I head to my room to change. Trey's in front of me, giving me an exquisite view of his ass. That tux must have been tailored to fit his six-foot-four frame, and it does not disappoint. I'm a little sorry it's covered in paint now.

"I'll use the guest bathroom," he says.

"No." I slide past him when we reach the top of the steps. "I want you to be in mine."

His jaw clenches even as his eyes soften. "Okay."

People are laughing downstairs and out in the backyard. It makes me freeze because I'm stuck between excitement and something else. I don't want to get caught, but at the same time, I love the idea.

I just don't want it to be by my son.

"Better get moving," he growls in my ear. Trey's baritone is soft but demanding. My nipples instantly harden. "How about a push?" He bumps my ass with his groin, and a shiver of delight zips through me.

We make our way into my bedroom, and I shut and lock the door behind us. My heart's racing a mile a minute, my hands are clammy. Paint is smeared across my door from me shutting it. Great. "This is why I can't have nice things."

"It'll wash off," he says, already pulling off his bowtie.

I watch him undress. The desire to beg him to bang me against my dresser is strong.

"You look like you've got something on your mind." He slips out of his shirt, and I gawk at his abs. No man should look this good. It's too humbling for us mere mortals. "Erin." He places his hands on my hips and the memory of what we did in the hotel bathroom yesterday morning shoots through me, making my pussy ache. "Do I have to carry you into the shower..." Trey nips my earlobe. "Or make you crawl there?"

Oh. My. God.

Threats like that shouldn't make me so hot. But they do. They really, really do.

I somehow find two functional brain cells to rub together and put one foot in front of the other, eventually making my way into the bathroom.

I feel good when he treats me like this because I don't have to think, I just do what I'm told. And the way he looks at me, the way he touches me... I turn into a Goddess on the inside and out.

Until I catch my reflection in a mirror like I am now.

Holy moly, the bags under my eyes should require their own luggage tags. And my mascara is smeared from crying and from laughing too hard. There's paint in my braided hair and my boobs are spilling out of my top because the dress weighs more now that its saturated.

I look awful.

Desperate to fix myself, I reach around to unzip my dress and can't snag the stupid zipper. The more I try, the harder it gets. Damnit! Just as I eye up the drawer that holds a sewing kit and debate using the scissors to cut myself out of this damn thing, Trey's hand lands on my waist.

He cocks an eyebrow at me through the mirror I'm still standing in front of. "Did I tell you to take this dress off yet?"

Now isn't the time for his bullshit sexy talk.

"I'm about two seconds away from cutting myself out of this thing, Trey. If you don't help me unzip it, so help me God…"

He makes no move to help.

And I'm not bluffing.

Spinning on my heels, I march over and grab the scissors from my drawer. He pulls me backwards, sits on the bed, and turns me over his knees and takes my scissors away. I hold still, thinking he's going to spank me, almost desperate for it.

Instead, cool air hits my back as he unzips my dress. "Now get up and face the wall, Erin."

I almost don't want to. But whenever I follow his commands my head shuts off, and it feels good.

"Lift your arms," he says softly, but firmly.

I do and the dress pools down around my ankles, slipping effortlessly off my body to display the oh-so-not-sexy-or-comfortable shapewear I'm wearing underneath it. My face heats and I want to crawl under a rock and die.

"What is this?"

"What's it look like?" I snap back at him.

Trey rises from the edge of my bed and makes his way to me in three strides. He lifts my chin with his finger. "Do you like wearing it?"

His question catches me off guard. "I like looking sexy," I admit. "This helps me achieve that."

But it kind of hurts and is uncomfortable since I'm not used to it and it's probably a size too small at this point.

"That's not what I asked you, Erin." He slips his finger under my shoulder strap, toying with it while his other hand spans across my ribcage. I can't even feel him touch my side because the fabric is too thick and tight. "Do you like wearing this or not?"

"No," I confess. "But—"

"Shut that pretty fucking mouth." He moves in front of me, holding the scissors between us, and runs the sharp tips down between my breasts. I'm breathing fast, which makes my hefty chest rise and fall.

I'm not afraid of Trey. I'm afraid of how much I'm going to like what he might do next.

He tugs the crotch of my shapewear and cuts it. The straps instantly stop digging into my shoulders, giving me a little relief. I'm about to say something when I suddenly feel him pull the front of the shapewear down, stretching it taut as he cuts it up the middle.

"You think squeezing and reshaping will make you look better?" His tone is sharp.

It makes me hotter.

"I think it smooths out the lumps which is nice." My cheeks burn with embarrassment. My heart's in my throat. This is thrilling and humiliating and relieving all at the same time. I can't tell if I want to cry or kiss him.

"You wear shit like this only if you want to, not because you think you have to. Understand me?"

I swallow the lump in my throat. "Yes."

Goosebumps ripple down my arms and legs when he touches my belly with the back of his hand. I hate that I'm not fit anymore. I hate that I have a scar from my C-section and a bunch of stretch marks. I hate a lot of things about myself, but when Trey talks like this, it gives me a distraction. A skewed view. He touches me like I'm a sculpture behind a big red rope he's not allowed to cross and does anyway.

"Now," he says, nuzzling my neck as he pulls the tattered clothing off me. "Get in that shower so I can make you twice as wet."

• • •

"I'm going to give you one minute to get dressed in an outfit you love to wear. You will not put on underwear. You will not put on shoes. And you're going to meet me in the hallway before your minute is up. If you don't, I'm coming back in here and you won't like what I'll do." He nips my bottom lip. "But I will."

My eyes roll back and lashes flutter.

I honestly can't tell if that's a threat or a promise.

And I have no idea what's gotten into him.

But when Trey leaves and shuts the door, I swear I start counting in my head and rip into my closet like my house is about to crash down around my ears. *Something I love to wear. Something I love to wear...*

I don't have anything! Every pair of jeans, shorts, and all my dresses don't hit right.

I'm running out of time.

I can't believe I'm this giddy to obey. I can't believe he's being so bossy! I can't believe I'm panicking about screwing this game up, because what's the worst thing he could do, come back in here and blow my back out? Oh darn.

But Beetle's downstairs with Glitch and Ara and I have a lot more guests in my house that I need to remember are going to be here for a while. There's a time and place for the game of "Almost getting caught." Right now isn't it.

I jerk the hangers around and finally find something that might test Trey's tolerance. With a devious grin, I slip into the blue sundress and pull my hair into a low ponytail.

Trey telling me to wear something I love and calling me out on that shapewear under my dress makes me feel some kind of way. Shame doesn't hold a candle to my confidence right now. Because this *is* an outfit I absolutely love to wear.

Is it fancy? No. But it's still cute and my boobs look pretty damn great. I dash to the door, and hear Trey's low, rumbling, soft voice counting down on the other side. "Six… five… four…"

I jerk the doorknob and swing it open.

Trey stops counting and stands straighter, pushing away from the railing. His gaze drags up and down my body, a smile spreading across his handsome face. He even bites his bottom lip, before saying, "Oh, we like that."

Yes. We. Do.

Trey always looks at me like I'm the sexiest thing in the room. It makes me feel hot instead of frumpy. Sashaying past him, I grab a hunk of his shirt to pull him with. "Let's get downstairs before someone notices we're missing."

He catches my wrist before I make it very far. "You've disobeyed me."

The hell I have. I throw my hands up. "Not funny, Trey."

"Am I laughing?"

Yes, he is with his eyes. They're light and filled with humor and lust. Trey starts pulling my sundress up, and my breath catches when he grazes his knuckles across my panties. Arching his brow, he growls, "I said no panties."

"We're having a wedding down there!"

"I don't give a fuck if it's the second coming of Jesus down there. I said no panties."

Did I know he'd have this reaction to my little disobedience? Sort of. I didn't expect it to make me feel this hot but hey, my ass isn't going to spank itself.

He slides his hand down, taking my underwear with him.

Using his shoulders to balance myself, I step out of the blue panties, my cheeks flaming with excitement.

He brings them to his nose and inhales, deeply.

I watch him do it and I get so wet, I'm certain it's dripping down my legs. "I can't go down there like this."

"You can and you will." He slaps my ass, making me yelp, and leads me to the steps. "Naughty little slut."

My cheeks burn with embarrassment and elation. I don't like being called a slut.

I love it.

Walking down the steps, I give him a spectacular view of my ass and bite back a squeal when I hear him groan behind me. I can't believe how empowered I feel in a stupid sundress and no underwear. It's naughty and risky and exciting and dirty. Here's hoping I don't leave a big, noticeable wet spot on my chair at the reception, but even if I do, I think Trey would have some way to make me feel proud about it.

My bare feet hit the bottom floor and I look up to see him still staring at me from the top of the stairs. Gripping the banister as if trying to hold back from something — like hooking this dress over my ears and taking me every which way I beg him to — he licks his lips and shakes his head. "*Damn.*"

With a fuck-ton of confidence, I flash him a grin. "You coming?"

I don't hang around to hear his answer.

He'll be coming alright.

Later tonight, I'll make sure we both do.

Chapter 13

Trey

The reception tested my willpower for five solid hours. The amount of times I wanted to sneak off with Erin is a new record. I thought about fucking her behind the shed. Eating her pussy in the laundry room. Take her upstairs and breaking her headboard—all before the cake was cut.

I fingered her under the table twice. Used her panties to wipe my mouth with after taking a sip of my champagne. It drove her wild nearly as much as it made me feral. To have the scent of her cunt so close and not being able to have it?

Torture.

When she danced with Glitch, I played UNO with Beetle and snuck him an extra soda. At one point, he and I snuck off to play catch behind the shed.

The whole night was magical and ended with me going back to my hotel room alone. She didn't offer for me to stay with her, and I didn't ask. I get it. She's guarded for good reason. Erin's thinking about more than just herself and is being cautious and protective. Beetle's gone without a father his entire life, and although Glitch is an amazing stand-in, he's just an uncle.

And I'm just his uncle's best friend.

Is it wrong that I want to be more for that kid? I mean, I've always treated him and Erin like my extended family, but the more I think about it, the more I want to have them both as my immediate family.

Erin might run like the wind away from me if I confess that to her. As far as I know, she's never even brought a guy home to meet her son before, let alone considered getting married and having a bigger family.

That's why I said I'd come back to the hotel tonight. I thought it would be good to give her a little space. And I'm sure she'd have suggested it too, if only for Beetle's sake. I have no clue how to navigate telling him about Erin and I. Ultimately, that's on her, as his mother, but it takes a lot of control to not make premature promises to a boy I wish was mine.

Tonight is that dinner with just the three of us. But the fun started earlier today because Beetle asked about my hotel room and if the place had a pool. Then he begged his mom to take him swimming and of course I was all for it.

So now, here we are, swimming and playing basketball in the hotel pool.

"Boom!" Beetle shouts. "Two points for me!"

"How is it you get two points for every basket, and we only get one?" Erin splashes him in the face.

"Because you're bigger than me." He splashes her back. "You have an advantage."

I laugh, grabbing Erin and hauling her back. She squeals and kicks as I call out, "Dunk another!"

Beetle slam dunks the mini basketball while I keep Erin locked in my arms.

"Cheater!" Erin laughs. "You can't sabotage our team to give him the edge!"

We splash and chase each other around while Beetle climbs out of the pool with the ball again. Before I realize what he's up to, he's backed way up.

For a running start.

"Watch this!" He books it towards the pool's edge.

Erin yells, "WALK-WALK-WALK!"

But it's too late. Beetle shoots off, ignoring his mom's warning, and beelines towards the pool with enough momentum to blast a rocket into space. He slips.

And catches the concrete with his face.

"Oh shit," Erin whispers, rushing to the side of the pool to climb out.

Fear grips me. I swim towards him and climb out of the pool right in front of Beetle just as he lifts his head.

Blood. Everywhere.

Erin runs to us. "Oh my god! Brendan!"

"I'm okay," he says, completely lying.

His front tooth is chipped, his lip is busted all to Hell, and his chin's got a nasty scrape, plus his nose is bleeding.

Erin snags a towel and holds it to his mouth. She's keeping calm better than I am. I want to rip this concrete up and replace it with soft rubber. In fact, I want to wrap this boy in bubble wrap so he can't get injured ever again.

"Let me see," she says calmly, wiping the blood off his face.

He's bright red, tears welling in his eyes. "I'm okay."

"Let me just make sure you didn't break your nose or split your chin and need stitches." Erin tips his head back and I feel dizzy. I don't want this boy to hurt. Ever. And I'm well aware that kids get busted up all the time. Shit, Beetle's nothing short of a daredevil, but seeing him hurt makes my stomach plummet.

"It's not broken. I think you just knocked it pretty good. Most of the blood's coming from your mouth. Let me wiggle your teeth."

I hold my breath as she checks to make sure none are loose.

"You're good." Erin tucks him into her arms. "I'll call the dentist and make an appointment to have your tooth fixed."

"Am I gonna miss camp?"

Seriously? *Camp*? He's worried about camp when I'm more concerned he needs stitches and X-rays.

"We'll see," is all Erin says before kissing his head.

"Ugh, Mom. Stop with the PDA."

He says it like he's embarrassed about his mom smothering him with love, but I can see the way he's got his head buried against the crook of her arm, face cast to the floor as tears spill, that he's more affected by the audience watching us.

"Here's the first aid kit," someone says behind me.

"Thanks." I take the box and open it. There's no lifeguard on duty and I'm not even sure what I need out of this useless container to make my boy feel better. A band aid and ointment won't cut it.

"I guess we better get going," Erin sighs.

"I don't want to leave!" Beetle pulls back. Blood is smeared all over Erin's bathing suit and shoulder from his face. Poor kid looks like he was just in an MMA fight and lost. "Please, Mom. I'm fine. I want to stay. You said we were going to that new Mexican restaurant! You promised!"

"We can go another time." She wipes his hair back from his eyes. "I think we should go."

They stand up and my heart clunks in my chest. For the life of me, I'm not sure what to say or do. Getting busted up is part of being a kid.

Getting sick over seeing a child get busted up is part of being a parent.

Erin might be acting cool, calm, and collected, but if she's anything like my own mother, she's also mentally calculating the dentist bill, how to coordinate getting an appointment and getting him to camp so he doesn't miss much and is probably beating herself up for a bunch of other things — none of which are really her fault.

I want to help take some of the pressure off her. "How about we go up to my room and I'll get an ice pack and medicine from the lobby. We can chill for a while, maybe watch a movie, and see how you're feeling afterwards." Beetle beams me a huge, chipped-tooth smile. Holy shit, almost half his front tooth is completely gone. Did he swallow it? "But it's up to your mom, okay? Whatever she decides, we gotta respect it."

"Deal." Beetle looks up at Erin, waiting for her answer. "Mom?"

Exhaling, she cups her boy's face and inspects it again. "Well..." Erin frowns and tilts Beetle's head, "I guess since you don't need stitches, if you really — "

"YES!" He fist bumps the air before she finishes her sentence. "I've never been in a hotel room before!"

I watch Erin's shoulders sag. "Well, here's your chance, Evil Knievel." She glances over at me with a tired smile. I know exactly how she feels. All that adrenaline just shot through us and in a matter of minutes we've gone from fully loaded to depleted.

Survival mode, am I right?

When Beetle heads over to where we've piled our towels and their bag, Erin tucks a piece of hair behind her ear and says softly, "Thanks."

I don't know what she's thanking me for. "I've got you." I want to kiss her. Hold her and let her know that I mean it with every fiber of my being. "I've got both of you."

"Come on, guys!" Beetle loads his arms up with all our stuff.

I can't believe how fast kids bounce back. The number of times me and my brothers got hurt growing up was insane. It was also no big deal to us. This might be the first time I'm reflecting on how the hell my parents survived raising five boys. "I swear I almost had a heart attack watching him go down." His damn head bounced when he hit that floor. I can't stop reliving it in my head.

"Life flashes before my eyes every time he tries a new trick." Erin chuckles. "You'll get used to it."

I don't think I ever will, but damn if I don't want a chance to try.

Chapter 14

Erin

Monday's come way too fast. I'm running around this the morning like a chicken with her head cut off. I was able to talk to the dentist right when they opened, and they agreed to squeeze us in at nine-thirty. I know what "squeeze in" means. Beetle could be seen right away, or we'll be sitting and waiting for a while. Either way, I'm stuck and at their mercy.

Normally I wouldn't mind so much, but today's different. I have two job interviews and one's at ten-thirty, the other is at one. I'll have to take Brendan with me to at least the first one, because there's no way I can drive him to camp after getting his tooth fixed and still make my interview in time.

"Where's my damn deodorant?" I can't find it anywhere! I know I left it... Oh. Here it is. Right where I left it.

"What are you so dressed up for?" Beetles asks at my door, rubbing his eyes. His hair is sticking out at all ends, and he's got sheet crinkles on his face.

"Hurry up and get dressed. We've got to leave in fifteen minutes!" I woke him up three times already, and he fell back asleep every time! Grrrrrr. "Come on, dude. Mommy's got interviews, and you've got the dentist and camp!"

His chin scrapes and nose don't look nearly as bad today as they did yesterday, but it still hurts to look at. I hate it when he gets hurt. I wish I could take all his injuries onto myself and spare him.

Just as I'm scooting Brendan out of my bedroom, I hear my front door open, and slam shut. "Hey!"

It's Glitch. "We're up here!" I have no clue why my brother is here, but I don't have time to hang out. Grabbing a hair tie and shoes, I dash down the steps to make something for breakfast.

"Whoa, you look nice."

"Thanks. Got two interviews today and—"

"Uncle Glitch!" Beetle comes down the steps half-dressed and hair's still a mess. "Check this out!" He proudly points at his face.

"Dang." Glitch leans down to inspect the damage. "How'd you do that?"

I know Glitch is probably remembering doing the same thing to his face when he was twelve. Our mom nearly fainted when she saw him come inside from skateboarding at the park.

Not only had he split his chin open, but his braces had gone through his top lip, and he chipped the same front tooth as Brendan.

"We went swimming at Trey's hotel yesterday and I slipped when I was running to do a three-sixty cannonball trick with the basketball."

Glitch's brows rise to his hairline. He looks over at me. "Swimming at Trey's hotel room?"

"We went swimming, watched a movie, and went out to dinner." I don't need that look from him. I don't need to explain myself to him either. So why is my belly twisting with unease?

Because you've been sneaking around with his best friend for two years and now he knows and hasn't mentioned it to you yet...

"About that," he says, sitting at the table. His gaze goes to Brendan for a second. "Hey, Beetle. How about you go upstairs and do something with that hair? You look like you licked an electric socket."

"I'll just put on a hat."

"Nope. A hat won't cut it, man. Do as I say and go wet your head and fix it."

Sometimes I don't know how I feel about Glitch telling Brendan what to do. He's not the dad, he's the uncle. But there are moments like this, when I'm scatter-brained and stressed out, that it's nice to have support and backup. I'll be the first to admit, I cave a lot with Brendan because I'm too tired to argue over things like messy hair and bad manners. Glitch usually balances the scales and helps maintain respect here.

When Beetle runs back up the steps, I grab a bunch of random leftovers out of the fridge for breakfast. I don't have time to cook. "We're in a hurry. I have to have him at the dentist at nine-thirty."

"Then I'll make this quick." Glitch leans forward and nails me with a death stare when I set a tray of random appetizers on the table. "Don't hurt him."

I feel my defenses kick in. The sheer willpower it takes to not frisbee throw this platter of crab rangoons and eggrolls at his head is unreal. "Shouldn't you be saying that to him, not me?"

"Oh, I have. But now I'm saying it to you, Erin. You're both important to me and I'm not about to lose one because of the other."

It hurts that he'd ever think he'd lose me. "Glitch…"

"I'm just going to say this once." He taps his finger on the table. "If you're playing with him just to have some fun, stop right now. Find another boy toy. If you're playing for keeps, then stay out of your own head and let him into your life."

"He's in my life! Christ, he's been in it since you brought him home from college, freshman year!"

Glitch shakes his head. "You know what I mean."

No. I don't. "This isn't your business. Stay out of it."

"Not on your life." He stands up and walks over to me, lowering his voice. "Trey loves you. If you can't see that, or if you aren't ready to commit to something of that level, then fine. That's your call. But don't string him along for another two motherfucking years because you're still floundering to understand why you should have nice things like Trey in your life. He deserves to be more than your dirty fucking secret, Erin."

Ouch.

"What the fuck, Glitch. He wasn't a sec—" I cut myself off because it would be a lie. I did keep Trey a secret. "I was afraid you'd be mad."

"You're a grown ass woman. It shouldn't matter what I think or how I feel. It's your life and your decision."

I'm too angry to even look at Glitch right now. How dare he come to my house and say this shit to me. I haven't strung Trey along. Have I? I mean, we had a mutual understanding. An arrangement.

I want everyone to know we're together now.

Shame hits me like a sledgehammer. He's right. I've been acting like Trey is my secret boy toy, and I hate myself for it.

"I get it, Er. You've been judged your whole life. I just never thought you'd put me in that group of assholes."

"I'm ready!" Beetle yells, coming down the steps with his hair soaking wet.

"Grab something from the table to eat and let's get going." I can't bring myself to look at Glitch right now. I can barely hold my tears at bay, and the last thing I need is to cry in front of my son and have him ask questions.

"Listen, I didn't come here to upset you. I came to put the yard back to normal." Glitch heads toward the living room to go out the back door. The caterers cleaned up everything, but I still have to put back all my patio furniture, the trampoline, and bike ramp. "If you need to drop Beetle off after the dentist, I can take him to camp so you won't be late to your interview. It won't take me long here and I have the afternoon off."

I close my eyes and the first tear falls. What would I do without my brother?

"That would be great. Thanks, Glitch." I step outside and head to my car. My hands are shaking as I pull out my key fob and unlock the doors, ignoring my cell phone when it dings in my purse.

"Hey!" Glitch calls out from the front door. "Good luck!"

I don't think he's talking about my interviews.

Chapter 15

Trey

When I returned to my apartment earlier today, I expected the familiar relief that usually comes with being back home. Instead, I feel irritated that I live here and hate how far away I am from Erin. It's annoyed me before, but never to this level.

First thing this morning, I'd sent Erin a text asking how Beetle's doing and if she got an appointment at the dentist, plus I wished her good luck on her interviews.

It took her a while to text me back, and the entire time, I felt like she might block me or something. Stupid, I know, but the space between us is growing again. I think it's in my head — fuck, I *hope* it's in my head — and not really true. Maybe it's just the routine she and I have with each other.

It's always been the same old thing: I visit, we hook up, I leave, she doesn't contact me and when I cave and call or text her, she's short and to the point. Then we don't make contact until I'm in town again.

What started as a fun, forbidden romance, has turned sour in my heart. I'm relieved Glitch knows about us. I'm happy Erin seems willing to give us a try, but...

Ding.

My cell goes off and I pull it out of my pocket.

Erin: Tooth is fixed! Waiting for interview #1 to start now. I'm nervous.

My smile splits my face.

Trey: You're going to kill it. They'll be lucky to have you.

Erin: Thanks.

She doesn't say more and neither do I. For the rest of the afternoon, I'm a machine with work. I crank out cover after cover and load them as pre-mades on my website. I check social media, schedule posts for the month, and announce in my newsletter and platforms that I've got a new selection of cover deals. Then I head right into my meeting at three pm with my boss at Interactive Pixel.

"Trey," my manager stands and walks over, hand stretched out for me to shake. "It's been a while."

"How was Japan?"

"Beautiful." He sits down and gestures for me to do the same. "Looks like life is treating you well."

Does it?

"Anyway," he waves off the small talk. "I wanted to meet in person with you today because I have a new business proposal I'd like to discuss. As you've already heard, we're starting a new line of games."

Yeah, I know. My youngest brother is a video game developer here and was thrilled to be chosen as a leader in the department. "Reid's excited about it. You've definitely kept him busy."

"Busy enough where he's negotiated a spot for you on his team."

I work hard to keep my expression impassive. I loved designing video games, but it's not where my heart is. "And, what exactly would I be doing?"

"All graphic designs for the campaigns. As well as some graphics for the games. I know you prefer to stay out of the development, but we think you'd be a great fit."

We, as in Reid and my boss? Since when has my little brother been high up enough to call shots like this?

Holy hell, when was the last time I actually talked to him?

"He works like a machine," my boss says. "I don't think he sleeps."

That's not a compliment in my opinion. Reid's a workaholic. In fact, watching how sucked into gaming he got is one of the reasons I stepped back. There's more to life than your job and it's easy to have no life when all you do is put in eighteen-hour days at an office. Then again, he's found his passion and is getting paid bank for it. Why yuck someone else's yum? "I'm glad he's an asset to you."

"As are you, Trey. Those designs you made for the rollout of Screaming Falls have impacted our sales tremendously. We've started a line of merch because two of your designs are trending already."

That feels… great. And premature. The game hasn't even officially come out yet. I had a demo of the game I shared with Beetle this weekend, but that's on the down low. I'm not supposed to share that shit with anyone. He loved it, but he's not the target audience.

"I know you said you wanted to step back a bit to focus on your other business," he hedges. "But I'm willing to offer you a significant bump in pay if you tag team this new line with Reid."

My knee-jerk reaction is to take it. A chance to make more money has been a goal of mine for a while.

But not necessarily in this industry.

"I'll consider it," I say cautiously. Then he shoves a folder across the desk with my offer inside. I flip the open the file and take a peek. "That's a lot of money."

It's also going to be a lot of dedicated hours in the office.

If I take this, I'll be living incredibly well. If I take this, I'll be working until I drop. If I take this, I'll get to spend time with my little brother and have new chances to expand my creativity. If I take this, I'll be back in the office instead of working from home.

And the office is the last place I want to be.

"You have until Friday to decide," he says. "After that, I'll be offering it to someone else."

I get the feeling I'm the first choice because Reid made this a stipulation as part of his contract. It would be so like him. My little brother will always try to sweep others into his success if he can.

"You'll have my answer by Friday." I get up and shake his hand again. Plucking the folder from the desk, I swear I float out of the office and once I'm outside, my first instinct is to tell Erin about it.

Then I pause. Shit. She'll likely see this as too much too soon. Maybe she'll think I'm smothering her.

Bitterness burns in my stomach. I should be able to share anything with her whenever I want. If she thinks I'm being too much, then she can go find less. Fuck it.

I pull out my phone just as it goes off. I'd put my cell on silent for the meeting and it looks like I've missed several messages.

Erin: Interview #1 suuucked. They couldn't offer me full-time for the six months, which means no health insurance. Ugh. That's not what they advertised. Glitch stopped by. He's taking Beetle to camp for me. Thank fuck, since it's on the other side of town.

Erin: Am I being annoying? Sorry.

Erin: Did you have that meeting yet? What did it end up being about?

Erin: Holy shit, I'm being annoying, aren't I? I suck. I'm sorry.

Erin: Just block my ass when you get sick of me.

Wow. This is very different from the past two years with her. She's never texted this much. Ever. It lifts some of the tension from my shoulders.

Trey: Boo for Interview #1. Glad Glitch could take Beetle to camp for you. Meeting for me was interesting. I'll tell you about it later tonight. Good luck with #2.

I want to tell her to make sure she eats lunch. But I don't. I also want to tell her that I miss her. But I don't.

Erin: Can't wait to hear about it!

She then sends me a selfie of her in the car eating a burger.

Erin: Not the meat I want, but it'll have to do.

I laugh.

Trey: What kind did you want?

Erin: A footlong *wink emoji*

Trey: I only have nine inches to feed that pretty mouth.

Erin: *sighs* I miss it already.

Trey: Then I'll make sure you don't miss it for too long.

She doesn't respond and I force myself to let the conversation go.

The rest of my day is spent on the phone with authors and also my realtor, surprisingly. I'm not sure if it's the universe telling me something or not, but I've been looking for ways to diversify and decided flipping houses could be a lucrative path to take.

Guess it's in my blood.

My dad owns a construction company and can help if I need him to. I don't mind doing most of it myself, but I'm no professional. I figure whatever work I can't do, I'll hire a general contractor to handle. Growing up, my dad always made us work summers with him, so I'm no stranger to drywall and floor installation, but the places I'm thinking of investing in are far away from where I live.

I stare at the folder on my coffee table. If I accept this offer, I won't have time to flip houses. I also wouldn't need to for the extra income. There's a lot of money in this opportunity for me if I choose to accept it.

But is this job what I really want to spend my time doing? I love the company I work for, but I think it's because they let me set my own hours and I can do my thing with no one breathing down my back. If I take this new position, I'm not sure the dynamics would remain the same. Actually, I'm ninety-nine percent certain they won't.

The thought makes my stomach drop.

I've grown used to setting my own hours. I love taking my work with me wherever I want to travel and cranking out my projects in the middle of the night and early morning. I'm more productive when I set my own pace instead of going by a corporate clock.

Leaning back on my couch, I glance around me and miss Erin. My apartment is nothing like her house. For one thing, my place is extremely modern. Black leather furniture in the living room with a glass and iron coffee table in the center. Off to my right is the kitchen and the back wall serves as the focal point with a counter-to-ceiling marble slab. My bedroom has light gray walls, a black headboard, white bedding, and dark flooring. The focal point there is a painting I bought from a street vendor a year ago. It's of a naked woman's back, her ass on full display as she ties her hair up.

It's the flare of the hips for me. I bought that piece because it reminded me of Erin. Not that I'll ever admit it to anyone.

Erin's beautiful body is a series of pleasure points for a man like me to sink his teeth into. My mind swirls with thoughts of spreading her thighs wide and licking her until she's screaming my name. That woman is addictive and I want another hit... badly.

My cell goes off, snatching me out of my fantasies.

Well guess who it is. "I was just thinking about you."

"Oh yeah? Thinking about how I'm turning into a bugaboo already? I'm shocked you haven't blocked me."

I would never. "I was actually thinking about how you're built to fuck."

"Ohhh, perv. Maybe *I* should block *you*."

She would never.

I laugh and relax against my couch. "So, how was interview number two?"

"Not too awful. They said they have more interviews to conduct so, I'll take that as not promising."

"You never know. They just have to do their due diligence and make it fair for all candidates."

"I'm honestly not going to be heartbroken if I don't get it. The pay is crap, but it has decent benefits."

My heart clenches that she's struggling at all. My job has incredible benefits, and it sucks I can't share them with her.

"It's okay," she says. "I lucked out with my severance package, so I have time to keep hunting. I've really got my hopes up for the interview this Wednesday. It's with a real estate firm, so I'm already qualified since I worked at one for several years. It's a desk job though, which means I'll be right where I picked up at my last job. Anyway, enough about me. What happened with you today?"

I can't even believe this is the same woman I've been low key in love with for years. She's talking like we've had a million phone calls between us already. News flash: We haven't.

Part of me inwardly cringes because I don't want to throw my good news in her face when she's struggling for something similar and hasn't achieved it yet. But I know Erin well enough to understand she'd never get jealous over someone else's joy. "I got a job offer today."

"Really?" She sounds excited. "I didn't know you were looking for a new job."

"I'm not. It's with the company I already work for." My gut feels heavy. "They're opening a new branch and my brother is in charge of it. He's negotiated for me to join him."

"Reid's the youngest, right?"

"Yeah." I've never really discussed my family with her, so it shocks me that she remembers his name. "Reid's the baby."

"And then it's Cole, the architect?"

"Mmm hmm."

"Michael, the baseball player. Then you, and the oldest is…"

"Julian."

"Julian." I can hear her smile as she says his name. "He's into stocks?"

"Yeah."

"Wow. Your parents must be proud. All five of you have stellar careers."

Too bad a career doesn't make the man. "We've done pretty good. My parents were really adamant about us following our hearts."

"And Julian's heart beats for the stock exchange?"

"He's weird. Numbers speak to his soul."

Erin's laugh fills my ears, and it's contagious. "So, are you going to take it?"

"I'm not sure." My gaze sails to the folder again. "It's an incredible deal, but…"

"It doesn't speak to your heart."

"I don't know. Not gonna lie, the paycheck makes my dick hard."

"I bet lots of things make your dick hard."

Touché. "You, most of all."

"Oh yeah?" Her tone changes. "Show me."

I snap a pic of my hard-on and send it to her through text. Just talking to Erin about my day makes me want to fuck her.

"Jesus. That thing should come with a warning. And a safety harness."

I laugh so hard I start to cough. "You're great for a man's ego."

"Well, they can be pretty fragile. Don't worry. I'll handle yours with care."

"Like you do when you take my cock in that pretty little mouth?" She groans into my ear and I'm suddenly holding my cell so hard, I might just crack the case. "Keep making those noises, little slut, I'll have to drive all the way back to gag you."

She moans louder.

Damn her.

"Okay, okay, I'll quit. Knowing you, you're already at the door with your keys."

How'd she know? "Would you like me to be?"

There's silence between us. My hope wilts. More silence. Shit, did we get disconnected?

"Trey?"

"Yeah?" My hand is still on the doorknob. Because, yes, I'm willing to drive back to her tonight. Going all day without Erin felt like an eternity. How the hell have we managed to do this for two years? I can't stand the thought of doing it for one more night.

"Is it selfish of me to say yes?"

Holy shit. "You want me to come back to your house?"

"Mmm hmm. I know it's ridiculous and a lot to ask but..."

"I'll be there in two hours."

I was in her driveway in an hour and a half.

Chapter 16

Erin

This is exciting. Not sneaking-away-and-almost-getting-caught exciting, but when I see Trey's car pull into my driveway, a small squeak climbs out of my throat. I can't believe he drove all the way back here.

I can't believe I asked him to.

My smile is so big it hurts my cheeks as I open the door.

"Hi," he says, looking just as happy as I feel.

"Hi." I stare at him for a solid three seconds before grabbing him by his t-shirt and jerking him to me for a scorching hot kiss. I want to climb this man like a tree and fuck him so hard he sees stars.

"Damn, girl." He starts driving me backwards, into the house. "A man could get used to being greeted like this."

"I can't believe you actually came back."
"Why wouldn't I? You asked me to."
"Yeah but…"

Trey kisses me again. "No buts, Erin. I told you, if you want something, it's yours. If I can make it happen, I will. I've been waiting for this moment for two years."

Biting my lip, words cram in my throat and I'm happy they do. The insecure parts of me want to argue that I'm not worth the drive. He has better things to do. I'm being a pain in the ass, and he could find someone better than me to date.

Except when I'm able to get out of that mindset, I know that I am worth it. And, honestly, I'm a catch.

A hot mess. But still a catch.

"I've been waiting for this moment for two years." I can't believe it's taken me this long to get with the program. I'm so ready to take this plunge with him, I don't care if we're long distance or not. We can do this.

We *will* do this.

"How long can you stay?" I don't know why I'm asking, or what I hope to hear.

"For as long as you want me."

The word *forever* burns on the tip of my tongue, but like the other things, I won't say this either. "Beetle's sleeping. I have to drop him off at camp by eight-fifteen in the morning." This week's camp is just a daytime one.

Trey's eyes round. "He's here, now?"

"Is that a problem?" I feel my defenses start to go up.

"Not at all, but what if we're caught?"

"We won't be. He sleeps like the dead." I drag him upstairs to my room and shut the door. Then I lock it for good measure. "I missed you."

The deep creases in Trey's forehead fade, and he's got a huge smile again. "I've missed you too."

"Is that dumb? We just saw each other not even twenty-four hours ago."

"Come here." He pulls me over to straddle his lap and he grips my butt. "I fucking love this ass."

"There's a lot to love back there."

"Take off your pants for me." He's talking low and quiet, which makes his register a little deeper. It sounds sensual and lazy and I love it.

"Yes, Sir," I tease, standing up and shimmying out of my sweatpants. I play with the hem of my t-shirt, waiting for more orders.

"Turn around, let me see what's mine."

My cheeks heat. I love that he sounds possessive of me. When I give him a perfect view of my backside, I do him one better and shake it just enough to make things jiggle.

"God... *damn*," he says. "You are so fucking perfect. Now get up here and let me see that pretty pussy." Trey leans back on my bed and waits for me to obey his orders. Crawling up his body, I make my way to his face and hover. He runs his hands up my thighs. "Stand up and straddle my head."

Confused, I do as he says.

"Take that shirt off."

Ooookay. I toss it onto the floor by my pants and balance my feet on the mattress by his head and press my hands to the wall to keep myself upright. The last thing I want to do is fall and squish him.

"That's my good little slut." The bed shifts and I look back to see he's lowering his pants to pull out his fat cock. "Spread them."

"I… my legs are already spread." What's he want, for me to do a fucking split? Not happening.

"I mean spread those pussy lips, baby."

Oh. My. God. Is he serious? It feels vulgar and naughty to run my fingers between my folds and spread them apart.

"Like a fucking butterfly," he growls with satisfaction.

With my forehead pressed against the wall by my headboard, my feet on either side of his head, my fingers keep my cunt wide open for him, I *feel* like a pinned butterfly.

Exposed and lovely.

"Lower that beautiful snack down on my face. I want a taste of what I've gone without all motherfucking day."

The instant his mouth latches onto my pussy, my eyes roll back. His tongue is diabolical. And when he finds my clit and starts sucking it, I hold my breath and relish the way a climax creeps its way out of me. Holding his head, I ride his face, putting pressure where I need it. He sinks a finger into me and hits a pleasure point inside my body that makes my impending orgasm coil tighter. I look over my shoulder and watch him stroke his glorious dick and wish I could feel those piercings graze my clit again.

But I'm too close to coming to climb down now. His dick will have to wait.

He groans from between my legs as I ride his face. I feel like a queen being worshiped on her throne.

Trey shoves his face harder against me, nearly suffocating himself as he jacks off. Grunting, he shoves even harder against me, grinding against my clit with delicious friction. "Oh fuck," I whisper. "I'm gonna come."

He does that move again. And again. And again.

My entire body tenses, warmth spreads through my belly, up my spine and across my face and neck. I explode with a climax that leaves me gasping for air. In the back of my mind, I know I might be too loud, but I don't care. My cheeks tingle. I'm lightheaded. Lifting off his face, I try to give him a chance to breathe.

He locks me in place, grunting into my pussy.

Still jacking off, he shakes with need. It's hard to get a good view with my back turned so I glance at my mirror on the side wall.

Holy shit, what a show.

Trey's long, muscular legs reach my footboard. His hand works his big dick and I'm not sure how it can feel good when there's nothing to lubricate it. He unlocks his arm from my thigh, releasing me, and I slide down his body. Our gazes lock. Trey's the most beautiful man I've ever met. I wonder if the butterflies I feel in my stomach for him will ever go away.

"Spit on my cock."

Jesus, the way he orders me around is amazing.

I work my way down his body until I'm hovering over his big dick, letting saliva collect in my mouth the whole time. Then I spit on his head, and he uses is to slick his length.

"Now get up here and suffocate me with that pussy, baby."

He doesn't need to ask me twice. Climbing back up, I stop just where my tits are in his face. "Suck first," I nearly growl.

He takes my left nipple into his mouth first and bites it just enough to make my breath catch. Then he goes for my right breast, sucking as much of it into his mouth as he can. Then he slaps my ass and shoves me upwards so I know to keep climbing until I'm back on my throne.

I smother him. Like, full on, take his damn breath away, smother him.

I hear him beat off, feel his arm snake around my leg to hold me in place, and when I look down, I can barely see his face between my thighs.

We stay like this long enough for me to actually worry I just might kill him if I don't pull off.

I rise.

Well, I try to, but Trey's arm on my leg locks me in place. He clings to it like he's desperate. Then he groans and his hips kick up.

I feel robbed of the show. I can't see him come from this angle and damn, do I wish I could watch. He taps my legs twice and I lift off instantly. Trey sucks in a ragged breath.

"Holy shit, you really couldn't breathe?"

"I can now," he says, still panting. "That was fucking amazing."

"I'll have to take your word for it. I missed the show, facing the wrong way."

"Well then, spin the fuck around and get back on here."

He can't possibly go again. I swear I don't know how his body pumps enough blood to keep his big dick so hard. But there's no way he can come again. Can't guys only do that once?

"Don't make me repeat myself, Erin."

Okay, fine, if he thinks he can go again, who am I to refuse?

Turning around so we're in a sixty-nine, his dick is now smack in my face. I run my fingers up his shaft, feeling his piercings, one-by-one. "I love these." I wish I could feel them without a condom, but I'm not risking it.

"Lower my meal down to my face. And when I tap you, put your tongue out for me."

Huh? I tilt my ass down and he wraps one arm around my lower back, locking me in place again. "Enjoy the show, baby."

I hold the base of his dick while Trey uses his cum as lubricant and starts stroking again. Meanwhile, his tongue is fucking my pussy and I nearly go cross-eyed with how good it feels. My body is super sensitive and I'm not kidding when I say this is the best porn I've ever watched.

He works the tip of his cock in little strokes and before I know it, he stuffs his nose and mouth in my cunt, and taps my leg twice. I barely remember what my orders are and miss the first squirt. Then I hold my tongue out for him to bust his load all over it and the rest of my face.

Trey tastes sweet. Always has.

He body bucks as he wrings every last drop from his cock and I hold steady so it hits me everywhere. Then I lift off his face and look at my reflection.

I love what I see.

"So damn gorgeous," he growls, smearing his thumb across my bottom lip. "Lick it clean." Trey gathers the cum off my cheeks and nose and chin, then shoves each of his fingers, one by one, in my mouth for me to suck on. "Now clean my dick off."

My heart slams against my chest as I obey.

Once I'm done, he kisses me again and then I slip out of bed to clean up. When I finish washing my face, I look at myself in the mirror again, and I feel different. I feel cherished and sexy, which doesn't make sense, but whatever.

I love being dirty with this man. I love that he's always pushing me to try new things and explore new kinks.

"Come over here," he crooks his finger at me.

I pad over to the side of the bed, and he grabs my arms and lifts me up so I'm laying across his chest, my head now buried in his neck. Our hearts pound together, his cock is between my legs and if I move a little, I know I could come again by rubbing myself against him. But I don't. Instead, we just lay together and he holds me. "You did so good, baby."

I didn't do anything. He did all the work! But I think I know what he means. I did so good letting him have control. Letting him boss me around. Letting him have the upper hand.

I could one-hundred percent get used to this.

He cups my face and kisses me like I'm the air he breathes. I could get used to that too.

We lay in silence for so long, just cuddling, and I start to drift off. Trey gently rolls me over and it's not until I feel him leave the bed that I startle awake. "Where are you going?"

"We fell asleep," he whispers. "I don't want to sleep up here and have Beetle discover me coming out of your room in the morning."

I agree. "When can we see each other again?"

I can't even process the twist in my gut when Trey grabs his clothes to leave.

His brow pinches together. "I'm not going anywhere, Erin. I'm just crashing on the couch."

The twist in my gut eases, but a hole appears in my chest. He's right. Beetle shouldn't find out like this and I've never in my life brought a man, other than Trey, to my bed before. My son may sleep like the dead, but there's no telling what time he'll wake up and come downstairs or barge into my room in the morning.

Trey leans down and swipes the hair from my face before kissing my temple. "Get some sleep. I'll see you soon."

I love you. The words are on the tip of my tongue. But I don't say it. Not yet.

"I love you," he whispers, then leaves, and the door shuts softly behind him.

Chapter 17

Trey

I'm creeping halfway down the stairs when movement on the first floor makes me freeze.

Beetle's holding a glass of water, staring up at me from the bottom step.

Oh shit. Oh fuck. Oh shit, oh fuck.

"Hey, little man. You get thirsty?"

He doesn't say a word.

If looks could kill, I'd be pushing daisies, especially by the time he reaches the step I'm on. "Brendan…"

He shoves past me and stomps up the rest of the steps, goes to his room, and shuts his door quietly.

What the hell do I do? Talk to him? Tell Erin? I bust a U-turn and head back to her room. My plan burns to the ground when I hear her already snoring. *Shit.* Swiping my hand over my face, I'm seriously panicked about what move to make.

Okay. Let's rationalize this. He just went to get a glass of water. He couldn't have heard anything. We'd been asleep. And I could be creeping down the steps at two in the morning for any number of reasons, right? Like using the bathroom, which is upstairs.

Fuuuuck, this is bad.

I make it all the way to the sofa, praying when he sees I've slept on the couch, he won't suspect I've done anything with his mom upstairs.

Wait, do ten-year-old's even suspect shit like that? Brendan's not like most kids. He's grown up faster than his peers and is probably exposed to a lot of things online and in the gaming community. Not to mention school.

I'm going to puke.

Has he seen other men leave Erin's room before?

A growl tears from my throat at the thought. I don't think she'd bring guys to the house, but I don't know for sure. It wasn't my business before, and I know for a fact I'll be the only man she brings to her bed from now on.

First thing in the morning, I'll tell Erin about this so we can work up a plan together.

• • •

Spoiler Alert: I've overslept.

Brendan comes downstairs like an elephant stampede.

Erin scrambles after him. "Get your lunch bag from the fridge. We gotta go!"

I've barely wiped the sleep from my eyes when the door slams shut and I'm alone in the house. I stare around me, unsure of how I got this confused. I didn't get a chance to tell Erin about last night. I didn't even make eye contact with Brendan this morning. The two of them ran through the house like a windstorm and were gone before I could roll off the damn couch.

I debate texting her, but if she's driving, I don't want her distracted by looking at her phone. And there's no way I can call because, again, distraction while she's driving.

Maybe I'm overreacting.

Maybe I'm not reacting enough.

Twenty minutes crawls by and I've cleaned myself up, folded my blankets and stacked pillows into a neat pile on the couch. Just as I step out of the bathroom, I hear Erin in the kitchen, banging pots and pans.

Ummmm. Okay. She's in a mood.

And she doesn't look at me when I come into the kitchen. Instead, she starts cracking eggs in a bowl, and I can tell by her body language that she's on edge.

"Beetle saw me coming down the steps last night."

She beats the eggs with a fork.

"I didn't know what to say or do. He went past me and back to his room and shut the door without saying a word."

She dumps the eggs into a pan, and they sizzle loudly. "I know. He told me."

I'm not sure what I was expecting her to say. "What do we tell him?"

Her shoulders tense. "I already told him the truth."

"WHAT?"

"I told him you and I are going to try dating. I said that you'd tucked me into bed last night and then slept on the couch."

Okay, that's not a lie, it just isn't the whole truth. I'm relieved she omitted the details because no kid can afford that future therapy bill. "What did he say?"

"He didn't say *anything*."

And that's why she's so uptight. The eggs start burning because she hasn't moved them around and the flame is as high as it'll go.

Erin's voice wavers. "He seemed angry, sad, scared. I don't even know what he's feeling."

"Protective," I say. "He's feeling protective of you, as he should." I'd seen that glare he gave me last night. It reminded me of the same one Glitch sometimes makes. "When he gets home, I'll talk with him."

"No, I will."

"Erin."

"Trey, don't push this. He's *my* son. I'll talk with him."

Now she's being the protective one.

I lean against the counter, fighting the urge to hold her. I know she's upset, and it's my fault for getting caught, but Beetle needs to know about us. We can't sneak around him anymore. "Do you trust me?"

"What does trust have to—"

"It's a yes or no question, Erin. Do you trust me?"

"Yes, but—"

"No buts. You either trust me or you don't."

Her cheeks turn pink. "I trust you, but he's my son. *Mine.* I need to be the one to speak with him about this."

"And you definitely can. I'm asking you to let me speak to him first. Trust that I won't make false promises or tell him anything inappropriate."

She waves me off.

"*Erin*," I say with more authority. "I'm not taking away from your parenting. I'm not trying to step in as a parent either. But he's been raised not just by you but his Uncle Glitch too. And that boy gave me a look last night that is just like his uncle. I know how to speak to a man with that look."

"He's not a man. He's a child."

"Which is why I'll be cautious and sincere and won't say more than necessary."

She shakes her head. "I don't like this."

"I know." I don't either, but it needs to be done. "Just give me a chance to set things straight with him. Please?"

• • •

There aren't enough hours in the day to be a full-time parent, employee, grounds keeper, chef, and chauffeur. I don't know how Erin does this every day. We worked in her yard, cleaned the house, ran errands, I got some work done for both my jobs, and now I'm in the parking lot waiting for Beetle to get out of camp. He's all smiles and talking with some other kid, which warms my heart to see.

Last school year he dealt with some bullies. It's not easy to make friends, and he's had a really rough time fitting in. I'm happy he's got a few buddies at camp with him. I hope that means this next school year will be better.

Beetle takes one look at me and his smile drops. His head casts down and pace quickens. He storms up to me and glowers. "Where's my mom?"

"She's waiting for us at home. I thought you and I could use some guy time. How about we go on a walk?"

I expect him to say he doesn't want to. That he's tired from being at camp all day and wants to go straight home. Instead, he keeps his head down and follows me without saying another word.

I've never had him not happy and excited to see me before. I'm terrified he might hate me. "Look, I need to ask you something, man-to-man. If you say no, I'll respect it, because that's what a man does. If you say yes, I'll make sure you never regret it, because that's also what a man does."

I sneak a glance at him. When he doesn't say anything, I walk along and wait for his response. I get it. Right now, he's using his silence as a control, because he feels like he doesn't have any.

We're halfway around the block by the time he says, "Alright. Ask."

"How about we sit on that bench over there?"

Beetle nods and marches over to it, his short legs working twice as hard to keep up with my long stride. He drops down and crosses his arms.

"I wanted to ask for your permission to take your mom out on a date." He's not looking at me. "I think she'd have fun with me. No," I shake my head. "I *know* she'll have fun with me. Do you know why?"

Beetle doesn't respond.

"Because I'm going to treat her like a queen. Your mom is the most special woman in the whole world, and she deserves to be treated like the most special woman in the whole world."

He looks over at me then. I watch him swallow hard. I can't read the look on his face, but if my heart doesn't stop pounding, I might stroke out.

"Sometimes..." Beetle says, with enough venom to make me cringe. "She hides in her room and cries."

God... damn. "I'll do everything in my power to make sure she never cries because of me."

That's a promise I know I can keep. I'll never betray her. I'll never say a nasty thing to her. I'll never make her feel less or treat her badly. All because I call her a whore and slut when I fuck her, doesn't mean I won't treat her like a queen twenty-four seven.

"If you break her heart," Beetle stands up and gets in front of me, "I'll beat your ass."

I don't doubt it for a second.

• • •

There's still tension between us as we head home, but it's manageable. I have no clue if I've handled things right with Beetle or not, but I heard what he *wasn't* saying to me on that bench. He didn't want me to break his mom's heart... or his.

I'm desperate to get back to the way we usually are with each other, so on the way home, I buy flowers for Erin and snag a couple treats for later. "Rule number one, when dating the most special woman in the whole world, you gotta spoil her." I grab the flowers and bag of goodies and we hit the porch. "Here." I hand him the bouquet.

"What are you giving them to me for? I'm not dating her. You are."

"Well, when I take her out on a date, I'll get her flowers from me."

"Then why'd you get these?" He holds up the roses.

"Those are for the best mom in the whole world."

Beetle huffs a laugh and nods. Pushing the door wide open, he yells, "Mom!" I come in behind him and we both kick off our shoes. "Mom!"

Erin's out back, dirt smeared over her forehead while she tends one of her flowerbeds. "Out here!"

Beetle runs through the living room and out the back door with the flowers. I hear them mumbling and Erin squeals and the energy she gives this boy makes my heart swell. No matter what kind of day she's having, she gives Brendan the best of herself.

How can you not fall in love with a woman like that?

They come inside and I pretend I wasn't just watching them hug by uncorking the bottle of wine she has sitting on the counter. By the time I've poured a glass, she's in the kitchen with me, holding the flowers to her chest.

"*Thank you*," she mouths and grabs a vase from a bottom cabinet.

"Here." I take the vase from her and replace it with the glass of wine. Then I take the flowers from her other hand and tip my head towards the steps. "How about you go take a bath while I get dinner going?"

She looks at me like I'm speaking in tongues.

Maybe she's never had someone take the reins like this before. Or maybe she thinks I can't cook. Either way, "Go on, now. Dinner will be ready in forty minutes."

"What? Wait. No. I can make dinner. I was just about to pull out stuff for burgers."

"No problem. I'll make them. You go relax in a hot bath while I do."

She continues to gawk at me.

"Go, Mom. The hot water heater can make it. Unless you've just washed laundry?"

She slowly turns to Beetle and her mouth hangs open a little. "No. I didn't do laundry since this morning."

"Well then…" I nudge her out of the kitchen. "Go relax for a bit. When you're done, come on down in your comfy jammies and we'll eat burgers and watch a movie."

The way her face lights up is enough to make my knees weak. "Oh my god. Seriously?"

"I'll never lie to you, Erin."

It's not unnoticed that Beetle's watching this whole exchange. Good. I want him to see how happy I can make his mom. I want him to see that there's all kinds of things I want to do for them both. Even if these acts are small, they're still genuine. "Now go up there and have a nice bubble bath."

"I… I don't think I even have any bubbles."

I make a note to order a box of bath bombs and other things for her tonight once I get a chance.

"Here." Beetle grabs the dish soap from the kitchen sink. "These good?"

Tears fill Erin's eyes as she takes the bottle from him. "I guess I'll find out, huh?" She looks back at me, and I can't tell if she wants reassurance or encouragement or if she just needs one more push in this direction. "Are you sure you don't need help with dinner?"

"I've got all I need," I say, winking.

"Stop stalling, Mom. I'm starving. The sooner you go, the sooner we can cook."

Erin blows out a breath and turns on her heels. I watch her sweet ass disappear to do what she's told, and I smile in triumph.

That's a good girl…

Chapter 18

Erin

Wednesday morning starts at 5:30 when Trey and I fuck against the washing machine. I'd been too nervous about today's interview to sleep and crept downstairs to iron my outfit and Trey decided to take advantage of it.

I'm glad.

This man makes my head spin.

He shouldn't be staying in my house like he lives here, but I don't want him to go yet. Besides, last night was incredible. As if a hot bath, then dinner and movie wasn't enough to make me feel spoiled, Trey and Brendan also spent an hour playing that new video game Trey brought over the other day. Watching them together warms my soul—even if Beetle's acting a little guarded.

I get it. He's a cautious kid. I've never let a man in my house before and he's never known about any dates I've gone on, so this is a huge deal.

Bam-bam-bam-bam.

Trey fucks me against the washing machine, stealing my breath with how hard he pistons into me. The door's shut, but I'm scared we're going to wake my kid up. I just can't seem to find it in me to make Trey stop railing me.

"You feel so fucking good," I whisper, holding onto the edge of the machine.

"If you're still able to form words," he growls, swirling his hips before slamming into me again, "I'm doing this all wrong."

My eyes cross when he hits a deep spot inside me that's half-pain, half-pleasure. "Fuck. That hurts so good."

He clamps his hand over my mouth and presses my back to his chest. "Shhhh."

My body locks up as I feel my orgasm creep closer. He lets go of my mouth to squeeze my tits and pinches my nipples, then bites my shoulder. "God, yes…. Don't stop."

Growling, because I'm still talking, he snatches a pair of clean panties from my laundry basket beside us and stuffs them in my mouth. "Good girls know when to talk and when to shut up and get fucked. Are you a good girl?"

I shake my head no.

I'm not a good girl. I'm a bad one. I like pushing boundaries and breaking rules and being a rebel.

Probably because it's been so long since I've done any of those things.

I could easily pull the panties from my mouth, but I don't. I let him fuck me like this until I come so hard the room we're in wavers and my knees buckle.

Trey eases me onto the floor and fucks me with my belly smashed to the tile and it's dirty and exciting and exhilarating and deep. Holy shit, he's going to puncture my lungs with his dick.

"So fucking hot," he growls. "Taking my cock like this. Squeeze that pussy, baby. I want to feel you grip me."

I clench my cunt and his breath punches out. "Fuck yeah. Again. Keep squeezing my cock. Milk it. Make me come."

I pulse on demand for him. Wetness coats my inner thighs. Lifting my ass up a little higher, I wish I could see what this looks like. Trey's arms bracket my shoulders, caging me in as he fucks me. I can't slide across the floor like this, I can't move much at all.

"Squeeze that pussy for me."

I don't this time.

"Gonna make me beg for it?" He half-laughs, then bites the back of my shoulder. "Just know, you'll be begging much longer than I will for what you want next."

I don't want anything. I'm so sated, I couldn't come again no matter what tricks he comes up with.

He lifts off me a little and shoves his finger in my ass. I groan around the panties in my mouth. No sooner does he make it feel good, he pulls it out. I grunt in protest.

"You like that?"

He does it again. Oh my god. How is it going in there so easily?

My head's reeling.

"You're so fucking wet, I could shove my cock in your ass with how much cum you have dripping out of your pussy right now. You're soaked, slut."

I think I might come again.

"Now…" he rumbles against me. Pressing his finger against my tight hole, he shoves it in halfway and says, "Squeeze."

I do because I'm desperate to be overwhelmed and this combo might just be the chaos I crave. I clench my inner walls, which also clenches my asshole and I swear I pull him into me deeper.

He fucks me and I clench him until our bodies both lock and go rigid. I come again when I feel his dick pulse inside me. "That's my pretty little slut, make me come. You feel that? Feel my dick throbbing inside you? Stretching you? Filling you?"

I nod my head and grind my ass against him.

"You like being fucked like a whore?"

I nod again.

I think I like it too much because I'm already trying to figure out how we can get away with round two.

Trey pulls out and spreads my ass cheeks. I feel exposed and dirty and lovely. I like him looking. I like imagining his cum dripping out of me, making a puddle on the floor.

I pull the underwear out of my mouth and take in a deep breath. "That was incredible."

He slaps my ass before helping me stand. As I regain the use of my legs, he pulls off the condom and ties it in a knot.

"There's a trashcan over there in the corner."

He pulls out a used dryer sheet and wraps it around the condom first before disposing of it. "I'll take the trash out this morning."

There's no need, but I can see he wants to hide any and all evidence. I'm okay with that.

I grab my dress from the hanger and open the door to get out of the stuffy laundry room first.

Trey follows me and sits at the kitchen table while I make coffee. My body feels boneless and sore in a nice way. I think I could go back to bed. My eyelids are heavy.

He checks his phone, like always, and I wonder how he juggles his two demanding jobs with such ease. His fingers fly across the screen, responding to something. "I'm meeting my real-estate agent today at ten."

"Okay." I'm not sure why he's telling me.

"I was hoping you could come with me."

"Why?" Look, I'm glad we're spending so much time together, but I don't think it's necessary to be attached to the hip.

"I wanted your opinion on it."

That catches me off guard. "Why?"

I hand him a cup of coffee—black, with two sugars.

"I want to flip houses. I think. Well, I'm looking into it. It would be nice if I could get a designer's opinion while I'm at it."

I take a sip of my coffee to hide my expression. Part of me is flattered. The other part of me is wondering what kind of game he's playing here. "Isn't it a little early to consult an interior designer? You're just going to look at the property. Flipping it and decorating it are not the same."

"Sure, they are. Sort of." He pulls me onto his lap, and I wince when I sit because I'm a little sore. "I don't have the gift you probably do when it comes to looking at a house and seeing its potential."

"How is that possible? You're a graphic designer. You literally take a blank canvas and turn it into cool shit."

"I have concepts to work with, a jumping off point. Even with my book covers, my clients give me a vibe to work with or images similar to the aesthetic they're looking for. I just translate that into covers. It's not the same as looking at a wall and knowing if it needs shiplap."

I snarf my coffee. "Shiplap? Do you even know what that is?"

"Not a clue," he says. "But I hear it's a thing."

Bless this man. "Where is it?"

"An hour from here. In Grant Ridge."

"We'd have to drive separately. My interview is at one."

"I can take you from there to your interview."

"No. I want to go alone. I don't need a driver."

I feel him tense under me. I wish I could feel bad about it, but I don't. He's trying to help me but it sometimes feels like too much. We're going really fast here. That's dangerous.

"Okay. Separate cars."

I nod and take another sip of my coffee before climbing out of his lap. Pouring a little more creamer into mine, I use the breathing space to collect my thoughts. I'm happy he wants to spend time with me. I'm happy he's interested in my opinion on his investment. But…

"Why are you looking at houses up this way?" Grant Ridge is a good three hours or more from where he lives. He can't flip a house that far away and still hold down two jobs.

"I plan to live in it — if it's possible — while I work on it. Then I'll sell it and do it again and again."

"That sounds…" I pause for a moment. "Unstable."

"It'll depend on where the next house is after this one. If I even buy it."

"Why Grant Ridge?"

"It has a lot of development potential."

Yeah. It does. I remember my former employers discussing it before they were bought out and forced to get rid of all their employees. "How will you do all the construction and still work at the gaming company?"

Trey's brow furrows. "I'll have it covered."

I don't doubt that he believes that.

Leaning against the counter, I cross my arms. "So, you're going to jump between jobs, and houses, and also try to maintain a long-distance relationship with me and Brendan?"

He places his coffee cup on the table and glares at me. "Yeah."

I shake my head. This isn't going to work. I know he thinks he can juggle all this, but that's because he has no idea how stressful it will be. He's never flipped a house before. He's never had to be three places at once, I bet.

But I'm not going to shove reality in his face this morning. Trey's a grown man. If he thinks he can handle it, fine. We'll see. However, I'm already mentally preparing for disaster and heartache. I know a thing or two about being stretched too thin and having too much going on at once all while having other people depending on you.

I refuse to depend on Trey.

As I grab cereal from the top of my fridge, I feel my guard going up again.

Unfortunately, so does Trey.

"Give it a chance, Erin." He leans forward and rests his elbows on his knees. "That's all I'm asking."

I swallow hard and dump cereal into three bowls. "Okay."

I hope he's right, for all our sakes.

Chapter 19

Trey

I'm not sure what's going through Erin's head, but after this morning's fuck session and coffee talk, I feel like she's entertaining me instead of taking me seriously. I don't like it. Except on my solo drive up to the house I might buy, I take in everything she said and didn't say.

Maybe I'm biting off more than I can chew.

Not with her. Fuck that noise. I mean with trying to take on a third source of income.

I've always prided myself in being great at multitasking. I've never met a challenge I couldn't conquer. But am I spreading myself too thin with my goals, or has Erin's doubt in my abilities taken hold of my confidence?

Probably both.

I'm not sure how to address either of those things right now.

Pulling up to the house in question, I see my agent is already waiting for me. Erin gets out of her car, and I escort her to the front door.

The agent beams a stupid, fake smile at us. "Good Morning!"

Whatever. My mood is souring by the second because even the outside of this place looks dismal. But this is what I asked for, right? A fixer upper. A hot mess I could put back together.

"I'm Erin," my girl says, because I've somehow lost my tongue and manners.

"Erin, I'm Maxine."

Blah, blah, blah. I barely hear what they're talking about because my head's already reeling with issues I see and we haven't made it past the porch. When we go inside, I stay quiet and look around.

It's a fucking dump. Granted, I saw the pictures—all three of them that were posted, which should have been a red flag—but now that I'm in it, I'm even more inclined to run out and never look back.

I can fix broken things. I can slap paint on a wall. I cannot, for the life of me, figure out how I'm supposed to turn this tightly boxed-in wreck into a family home to sell at a premium price.

This is a mistake.

"This is incredible!" Erin beams inside the piece of shit kitchen.

"Most of what you see is original to the house." Maxine says, hugging her clipboard close to her chest. "It definitely needs a lot of TLC, which is why the price is so low."

"Oh my God, Trey, look at the yard!" Erin leans on the dark red linoleum countertop to look out the filthy window. "Can you imagine a pool over there, a big patio with a fire pit over there, and in the way back a raised garden bed? My god, this place is fantastic!"

I seriously have no clue what to say. Erin's dress rises up her thighs as she lifts herself onto the counter to see more. The back of her right heel slips off her foot. I'm afraid she'll topple over when she climbs down so I hold her waist. "I think we're seeing two different houses."

She puts both feet back on the hideous tile floor and beams at me. "Well, shiplap can fix it."

That makes me laugh.

"Hello!" someone yells from the front of the house.

I don't fucking believe it. Greeting my little brother at the door, I'm gobsmacked. "Cole, what the hell are you doing here?"

"Dad told me you were looking at a house at ten. He couldn't make it, so he sent me."

I'd asked my father to come take a look at this place with me, but he said he was slammed with work but would try his best to make it. Seeing my brother here makes some of the weight in my chest ease up.

"Well, what do you think?" I ask, tossing my arms up.

Cole looks around and then his gaze lands on Erin. "I think it's gorgeous."

I smack his chest. "The house, asshole. The house."

"What house?" Cole swaggers over, his gaze never wavering from Erin, and he holds out his hand. "Hi, I'm Cole."

"I'm Erin."

He takes her hand and kisses it.

I'm going to kill him and bury him in the backyard of this property. All I need is a fucking shovel.

"You're the architect," she says, still smiling.

Cole smacks me on the arm. "You told her about me? *Nice.*"

Erin tucks her hair behind her ear. "My brother told me about you, actually."

"Oh yeah. Who's that?"

"Glitch."

Cole backs up immediately. "Holy shit. You're Glitch's *sister*?" He cocks his brow at me. "Bro."

"How about you focus on the house and not my girl."

"Your girl?" Cole's gaze bounces from me to Erin, then back to me. "Okay, alright, I see how it is." He rubs his hands together, still staring my woman up and down. "So what are we working with?"

He better be talking about the house and not my queen's body.

"Trey's not impressed," my girl says. "But I say it's got huge potential."

"Huge," Cole repeats in a husky tone. "Huge is a good word. We like that."

I smack him upside the head so fast, I'm sure his teeth clack. "Stop flirting with her!"

"Okay, alright, damn." Cole winks at Erin, while still rubbing the back of his head. "He's just worried I'll steal you right out of his arms like I did his first girlfriend."

"She wasn't my girlfriend. She was our babysitter. And you didn't steal her, you threw yourself over the railing of the deck and landed on a rosebush on purpose to get attention."

"The things we do for true love."

"She was fifty. And our neighbor."

"Still true love," Cole smirks. "That woman made the best chocolate chip cookies I've ever put into my mouth."

I'm getting a headache.

"Really?" Erin clasps her hands behind her back. "So all it takes for one of you boys to fall in love is a good cookie?" She glances at me. "I'll remember that."

I can't hide my smile when she looks at me this way. "I don't need your cookies." *I'm already in love with you.* "I'm a pie guy."

"Pumpkin, wasn't it?"

She knows damn well it's pumpkin.

"With…" She saunters over and wraps her arms around my neck. "Extra…" She drags me down until our lips almost touch. "Cream."

Erin kisses me in front of my brother and Maxine, and my dick hardens immediately. When she pulls back, her cheeks are flushed, and I have no clue what to do about the monster in my pants. Maxine pretends to look out the window and Cole is quietly laughing at me. I take a second to readjust myself.

"Okay, let's get back to business," I say, slapping my palms together.

We spend the next twenty minutes going through each room and walking the property line. Erin's ideas sound great, as far as I can tell. Any time she has an idea she's unsure of, she defaults to Cole and his approval.

"It's not a load bearing wall, I don't think. So yeah, it can come down." He looks around the living room again. "That's a good idea."

"It'll open things up and bring more light into the kitchen. We can put an island over there with seating and storage. If we bump out the living room a bit and move the mudroom to the back of the house, we can probably fit the laundry in there too."

"Hell yeah. That'll work. Then there will be more space in the kitchen for —"

"A sunroom." They say at the same time.

Cole's smile lights up the room again. "Damn girl, where'd you come from?"

"I'm from a special part of Hell." Erin looks at her hand and wiggles her fingers. "Chipped two nails crawling out of there last night."

That makes us all laugh.

"Marry me," Cole practically begs. "Please, Erin. Be my wife."

I smack the back of his head again.

It doesn't deter him. "Imagine the magic we'd make on and off a construction project."

She laughs again. I know he's joking, which is the only reason I'm not strangling him. But I'm getting tired of it. "Stop wasting her time, Cole. She has a job interview to get to."

"I'll offer you one. Work with me. I'll pay whatever price."

Erin laughs again. "Wow. It doesn't take much to impress you, huh?"

"On the contrary, I'm extremely difficult to impress." Cole's tone changes and the humor starts fading. "Which is why I'm dead serious." He pulls out his wallet and hands her a card.

She looks at it, and I see her hands shake a little.

"No pressure or anything, but you've got an eye and, in this business, that's a big asset. This whole time you've made decision after decision without a second-guess. My clients would appreciate someone with that level of confidence. And your taste is…" he makes a chef's kiss. "I'm not blowing smoke here, Erin. My firm's hiring so if you want to move to the bay side and work with some of the best architects and designers in the business, give me a call and I'll set something up."

She looks at me and I can't tell if she's searching for permission or assistance or what.

"I'll walk you out," I say, steering my brother towards the front door. "Say bye."

"Bye!"

Cole puts on a show like I'm dragging him out the front door.

When we get outside, I'm two seconds away from punching him. "Stop flirting with her, dickhead!"

"What the hell are you thinking, hooking up with Glitch's sister? Holy shit, Trey." Cole's humor is gone completely. "Does he even know?"

"Yes, he knows."

"Doesn't she have a kid?"

"Yeah. So?"

Cole shakes his head. "I hope you know what you're doing, man. You better have a plan."

I do, but I'm not telling Cole about it. He'll blab to my entire family before I have a chance to set things in motion. "We're taking it slow."

"*Slow.*" Cole's not buying it. "You brought her here. Are you planning to buy this place for the two of you?"

"Hell no."

"So you really just want to flip it?"

"Yeah. And I asked her to come because she's good at seeing past the mess."

Cole shakes his head. "I wasn't joking about that job offer. Make sure she knows it."

My heart clenches because Cole's not close to where she lives. The bay is hours away from here. Speaking of which, "Did you seriously drive five hours to come here and look at this place on dad's behalf?"

"Fuck no. I was visiting this week and Dad told me about it. He was going to come but got called into a job last minute."

Because if a worker can't make it in, my father will step up and fill in the position himself. That man works way too much.

Says the man who's about to take on a third job.

"It's got good bones, man. It would be an easy flip. A lot of work, but manageable."

"Think I should put in a bid?"

"If you don't, I just might." Cole scratches his chin and looks at the outside. "Roof needs to be replaced too. What are they asking for this place?"

"Ninety."

"Offer sixty with no inspection and see if they'll take it."

I can't imagine they'd go for such a lowball offer, but whatever. "Thanks for showing up. I appreciate it."

"Mom's happy you're inching closer to home. She seems to think you'll be living in the house while you work on it."

"That was the plan." I look around and shake my head. I can't imagine living here while I work on it. "I guess we'll see."

"Reid said you got an offer to work in his new department."

My brothers talk too much. "Yeah."

Cole's eyebrows lifts to his hairline. "You think you can handle a new position at work, a house flip, and a woman like that who has a kid?"

A woman like that. I get in Cole's face. "What do you mean by that?"

Cole puts his hands up and steps back from me. "I'm just saying, she should get undivided attention. You're setting yourself up to give her barely any if you take all this on."

He's right, and I don't want to admit. "I'll handle it."

"Yeah, well, good luck." Cole pats my back as we hug goodbye and then I head back inside.

Erin's going on and on with the realtor about more ideas with Cole's card in her hand. They're both laughing when I cut the moment short. "Erin, can I speak with you?" I hate to be rude. "In private."

Her happy expression melts away to concern. "Sure."

"I'll be just outside," Maxine says, hurrying to the front door.

Once we're alone, I fight for breath as I close the distance between us. Before she can ask what's wrong and before I ruin anything by opening my fat mouth, I cradle her face and kiss her.

She instantly melts into my arms, and I realize I don't want to give this up for anything.

I also know I want to give Erin the world and I have no clue how to do it.

"Wow," she says, stumbling back a little. "What was that for?" Her breathlessness makes my ego puff out because I made her that way.

"I just couldn't help myself."

"Well, lose control more often." She wraps her arms around my neck. "Please."

"Since you used your manners." I kiss her again and this time, lift her up so her legs hook around my waist. I carry her into the kitchen and set her on the counter.

I'd give anything to fuck her right here, right now, but I didn't bring a condom. So I settle for the next best thing. "Tell me your ideas," I growl. "I want to hear them again." Skating my fingers up her dress, I slide her panties to the side and sink a finger into her pussy. Pumping slowly, I aim upwards to hit her g-spot. "Come on. Tell me."

Erin's already breathing heavy. Her nails dig into my shoulders as she clings to me while I fingerbang her in the kitchen while the realtor is within hearing distance away from us.

"Come on. Tell me." I add a second digit.

"Take… oh god… take down those two w-walls." Her lashes flutter while I pick up pace. "And… blue's nice. Paint. So paint. Such good… fuck…"

"Blue paint on the walls?"

"Huh?" She's spreading wider for me now. "Yeah. Walls. There's walls."

I bite my lip to keep from laughing. Then I make her come around my hand. "That's a good fucking girl." I pull out and suck my fingers clean. "When you get back from your interview, I'm fucking you until you pass out. Understand me?"

Erin nods, still trying to catch her breath. "Yes, Sir."

Not gonna lie. I like her calling me Sir.

We leave the house and I tell Maxine we'll be in touch. Then I kiss my girl once more and allow her to keep her panties on for once, even though I'm dying to keep them as a souvenir.

"I should be home by five-thirty," she says.

"Can I pick Beetle up from camp?"

Erin's brow furrows. "Glitch was going to get him for me."

"Is that a yes or a no?"

"I don't want to put you out."

"Is that a yes or a no, Erin?"

I know she's fighting the demons in her head that are calling her a burden. I can practically feel her guilt and trepidation squeeze the air out of the space between us.

"Yes," she says quietly. "I think he'd love that."

I grab her chin and press my mouth to hers, gently. "Thank you."

She turns away but not before I see her smile. "Wish me luck?"

"You don't need it," I tell her. "But I'll wish it for you anyway. They'll be the luckiest company in the world to have you."

And I'm the luckiest man because she's going to come home to me.

Chapter 20

Erin

I'm on cloud nine as I pull up to the building, twenty-four minutes early and ready to slay this interview. My mood is high and energy big. Looking at that house with Trey was a blast. Even on the way here, I've come up with a ton more ideas I can't wait to share with him when I get home.

After a quick touch up in the bathroom, I head to the third floor and march over to the reception desk to give her my name and let her know I'm here for an interview. Then I sit down and all the confidence I had five minutes ago spills out of me.

What if they hate me? What if I'm not a good fit? What if I botch this up somehow?

I text Trey and he's right there with all the right things to say.

Trey: You're going to nail it.
Erin: Then I'm going to nail you.
Trey: I love your authoritative tone. But I'm the one holding the reins here.

Erin: I'm not a horse!

Trey: Does that mean I'm not a stallion?

Erin: You're probably bigger than a stallion. God, what do you feed that monster?

"Erin?" A man calls out and I drop my phone on the floor.

Picking it up, I smooth my dress down and shake hands with not one, but three members of the Violet Realty.

What the hell kind of name is that for a company?

I follow three white-haired old men into a conference room, and something makes me feel uneasy as they close the door. Now is not the time to have insecurities. I know my way around an office like this. I also know quite a bit about real-estate, even if I didn't get my license. All because this is a lower-level admin position I've applied for doesn't mean I won't climb the ladder. And I know firsthand that a company this size can't operate without people like me on the ground floor doing all the paperwork.

"We're waiting on one more to join us, but I think we can go ahead without him," says the owner of the company.

Yeah. The owner. No pressure there.

They start firing off questions and asking me all kinds of things that I have brilliant answers for. Then they dive into my resume, and I shine for a while until I don't.

"You didn't go to college?"

I should be used to this question by now, but I'm not. Lots of people don't go to fucking college and still have great jobs. Not having a stupid degree doesn't mean I'm not qualified, or over-qualified, for this position. "No, I didn't."

"Sorry I'm late," a man says behind me. He rushes around the table with files in his hand.

It takes him a moment to settle in his chair and look up at me but when he does, the floor falls out beneath my chair and I drop into a black hole.

"Erin, this is Stanley Kutcher. He's head of our HR department here at Violet Realty."

We gawk at each other and I'm not sure who's more shocked, me or him.

I pull my shit together fast. "It's a pleasure to meet you," I lie.

He doesn't offer to shake my hand. I can tell the misstep earns him a glare from his boss.

"Violet is such an interesting name," I say, clearing my throat. I need to buy time until my head is back on straight. Had I known I'd be interviewed by my son's sperm donor, I might have not bothered dressing so sweet and approachable.

I'd have worn better armor.

"Violet is my daughter's name," the owner says. For the life of me, I've already forgotten his name. It's like all my panic and anger is narrowing down on Stanley's stupid fucking face and I want to crawl across this conference table and choke him to death.

"That's a lovely name," I manage to say with a modicum of honesty. It is a nice name.

Annnnd now I know why I feel so heavy and the air's been sucked out of the room. Violet is the name of Stanley's wife.

He works for her daddy.

"Here at Violet Realty, we pride ourselves on being more than a company. We're a family."

I can't breathe.

"Loyalty is important to us. As is spending time with our loved ones at home. In this packet, you'll see the layout of benefits, including three weeks paid vacation for all new employees, which will increase one day per month after your first year. Plus, we have—" he pauses for a moment. "Stanley, hand her the papers."

"That won't be necessary."

My heart clogs my throat as this cocksucker stands up and holds the files by his side. "The position has been filled."

"Oh!" His father-in-law gets flustered and I almost feel bad for the man because he has no clue what's really going on.

I could ruin Stan's life if I spilled the beans right here and now.

But I won't.

Not for his sake, but for my son's.
Brendan's never asked to meet his real father but I'm sure he will one day. Until that time comes,

I'm not putting myself, or Brendan, in a position where Stanley can have easy access to us or leverage on me by saying I ruined his life by spilling his secrets.

"I'm so sorry to have wasted your time," the man says. "Stan, you should have made us aware. Instead, we've all wasted time here."

"The decision was only just made. It's why I was running late."

Liar.

Stan's easy to read. His ears turn bright red, and his cheeks get all splotchy when he lies.

Beetle's the same way.

I keep my composure and stand first. Then I reach over the table and shake the owner's hand. "It was a pleasure to meet you."

I say goodbye to everyone, then I'm out the door first, heading to the elevators so fast, it's a miracle I don't trip. I'm so mad. So sad. So fed up and frustrated.

The elevator door opens, and I practically jump into it, then hit the *close door* button a million times. *Click-click-click-click-click-click*. It's almost shut when a hand slides in to catch it.

Why couldn't the door have severed Stanley's hand off? In horror movies, it happens. Why can't it happen in real life, damnit?

He stalks into the elevator with me and the door closes. "What the fuck are you doing here, Erin?"

"I applied for a job and got called in for an interview. What do you think I'm doing?"

"I think you're here to fuck with me." He gets in my face. "I think you came to see what you can get out of me now that you know I've moved back to town and make a lot of fucking money."

I spit in his face.

So unladylike, I know, but I'm not a lady. I'm Erin.

And I'll be damned if I let this piece of shit intimidate or belittle me. "I didn't know you worked here, and for the record, I don't care if you've moved back or how much money you have, I want *nothing* to do with you."

He has the nerve to laugh. "Yeah, right. This company is worth millions. And you knew I married the owner's daughter. You keep tabs on me."

I only caved and looked into him *once* on social media in ten years. It's how I found out he has three kids and a wife named Violet. It was enough to set me off, and I never did that to myself again. "Watch your tone when you speak to me, Stan."

"Get out of here before I call security," he growls as the doors open.

I step out but before I walk away, I rethink things. Spinning on my heels, I shove my hands on the elevator door to keep them open until I've said my peace. "I hope you know what you're going to say."

"Excuse me?"

"One day, Brendan's going to ask who his real father is. He may even want to see him. And the thing about my parenting style is I never lie to him. So if, and when, he asks me about you, I'll tell him everything. I'll tell him you didn't want him. That you threw money at me and told me to get rid of him. That you knew where he was all this time and never bothered to meet him."

No, I won't.

I'm not a heartless bitch.

I'll tell Brendan that his biological father was young and scared and didn't think he was ready to be a dad. I'll never speak about how he treated me then or how he's treating him now. Brendan can find out Stan's an asshole on his own if he chooses to meet him one day. I won't need to tell stories about his behavior, the bastard's actions speak for themselves.

"But what are you going to do?" I ask, seething. "When Violet asks why you never told her you have another child. Family is of utmost importance to the company, right? I'm sure your father-in-law will be thrilled to hear you have a child you've never met but have known about all along. And that you lied at his mother's interview and didn't offer her the job she's more than qualified to fill."

Stanley's cheeks turn brilliant red. He clenches his jaw, and his hands tighten into fists at his side.

"We've *never* needed you," I hiss at him. "And we never fucking will." I shove my face back into his. "Don't you wish you knew what it was like to have a fucking spine like mine?"

I do what it takes for the ones I love. I'll never stop being an amazing mother to *my* son. And I'd rather eat dog shit than work for this bastard or anywhere near him. There's something better for me out there. I'm worth taking a chance on myself and finding it, taking it… mastering it.

"I don't need this job," I say with confidence. "But *you* do. What's going to happen when your father-in-law finds out you're a liar and a snake? What's Violet going to do?"

He pales instantly. "You can't tell them."

My heart sinks knowing he's choosing to save his ass over doing the right thing. Then again, that tracks for this jerk. He did it the day I came to him, scared shitless, and told him I was pregnant. He probably does it every day at work. I always knew I was better off without him, and today just solidified that not only am I better off, but so is Brendan.

It makes a switch flip in my mind — the one that sometimes wondered on my darkest nights, what it would have been like if things were different, and Stanley had stepped up all those years ago. Back then, I saw a guy who had his dreams within grasp, and he pushed me away and ran from the consequences of our actions because he didn't want to be tied down or locked in with someone like me.

But someone like me is amazing and anyone would be lucky to have a woman by his side who isn't afraid of facing challenges and who loves with her whole heart. Confidence steels my spine and a smile spreads across my face.

"Have the life you deserve, Stanley."

I let the doors close while he's still turning the color of a tomato.

Then I leave the office and head home to my amazing family.

Chapter 21

Trey

Erin's home much sooner than I expect. I hear her car door slam shut and look out the kitchen window just in time to see my girl march around the side of the house to the gate. What the hell? I run into the living room and see her heading through the backyard and straight into the shed.

She comes out a few seconds later with a baseball bat.

My girl looks like she's ready to use it on someone's head.

I open the back door for her. "Erin, what's wrong?"

She shoves past me and now I can see she's been crying. Her eyes are red-rimmed, and the tip of her nose is pink.

I want to slaughter whoever has made her cry. "Erin. Talk to me. What's happened?"

She doesn't say a fucking word as she marches into the basement. I swear I feel like I'm in a twilight zone. "Erin!"

She storms over to the hot water heater and swings that goddamn baseball bat.

My girl hits it over and over. *Wham! Wham! Wham!*

She screams and cusses at it. *Bam! Boom!*

She kicks it so hard her shoe flings off. Then she kicks the other high heel off and starts swinging the bat again.

She's also starting to make some real damage.

Shit!

I grab Erin by the waist and haul her back, even as she screams and kicks. "You're going to make it explode!" I yell.

"Let it blow up! Let it all blow up! I don't care! I hate this house! I hate it!" She tries to hit the hot water heater again and ends up throwing the baseball bat at it instead because I won't let go of her.

Then she sags in my arms and starts crying so hard I can't make out anything she's saying.

I smooth the hair from her face. "Slow down, baby. Tell me what's going on."

"I saw him. He works at the stupid company! He lied and then basically accused me of stalking him."

I still. "Who?"

"Stanley."

"Stanley who?"

"Stanley, Brendan's f…" She can't even bring herself to call this man Brendan's father because he never was one.

"Okay." I get it now. There's no need for to explain further. I don't want her more upset than she already is, nor do I want her wasting energy on a piece of shit that doesn't matter. "How can I help?"

If she wants me to leave and give her space, I will. If she wants me to go kill the man, I will. If she wants me to hold her while she falls apart, I will.

"What time is it?"

"It's…" I glance at my watch. "Four fifteen."

She sags in my arms and lets me hold her. Why do I feel like she's only giving herself a fifteen-minute mental break before she gears up for the next thing on her to do list?

"How about we go for a walk?"

"I don't want to go for a walk."

"Then let's go sit outside and get you some fresh air."

She swipes the tears off her face, smearing her mascara and I'm so sad for her because I don't know what to do other than take her hand and lead her up and out the back door to sit on her patio. The sun's been swallowed by gray clouds, and I think rain is coming.

"Of all the companies in all the world, how did I have this kind of luck?" Erin starts crying again and all I can do is hold her.

"You'll find something else." And truth be told, my brother's offer was real. Maybe I can convince him to let her work on his behalf in this area? Even as I think it, I know it won't be possible. His company only focuses their business in the bay area. Erin would have to move and there's no way she'd go that far away from her brother.

Beetle would be devastated.

"I'm done," she says, pushing away from me. "I'm done being stuck. I'm done being mad about everything I couldn't control."

I brace myself for whatever she might say next. Instead, she leans into me and sighs.

"How can I help?" It's the only thing I can think to ask. I just want to make it better. Erin doesn't need fixing, but her water heater sure as shit does now. We're lucky it didn't explode.

Thunder rolls in the distance.

"Can you still get Beetle for me today?"

"Absolutely." I'll need to leave soon to make that happen.

"I'm going to the hardware store."

"That water heater can't be fixed, baby. You completely killed it."

"I'm going for paint swatches," she says, surprising me. "And carpet samples."

My brow furrows.

"I've got money to fix this place up. Whether I sell it or stay, I can't stand keeping it like this anymore."

I have no words right now. She needs control and change and if this is how she wants to handle it, I'm not standing in her way. "Would you like me to come with you? We can grab Beetle together, then pick out paint and maybe get a pizza for dinner?"

She shakes her head. "I need to be alone for a little bit."

My heart sinks. "Okay."

Erin reaches out and squeezes my hand. "Thanks for this."

A sinking feeling hits my gut as she gets up and walks away.

• • •

Erin

By the time I'm halfway down my road, it's pouring. Perfect mood setter. I'm stormy too. Brooding and dangerous, I'll feel like a hurricane once I get started on making my house different.

I'm sure this is just me projecting my shit show life onto drywall and hardwood, but I don't care. And though this is probably not the best time to begin such a huge project, I know if I don't start now, I never will.

Because I never have.

If I wait another day, I fear I might always live with my stained carpet and faded painted walls, and crappy sofa. I'll turn into an old shrew full of resentment and be miserable. And I may not be able to afford all the changes I've envisioned making to my house, but I'll at least get some of it done and that's a start.

I need to do it so I'm no longer stuck.

Rain pummels down and my windshield wipers do little to help me see. Turning my hazards on, I go slower and keep alert. The storm lasts for about three minutes then lifts a little. Thank fuck. I drive in silence with just the annoying rhythm of my wipers going.

Maybe I'll take Cole up on his offer. Maybe moving far away from here is what I need. I don't want to be in the same town or anywhere near Stan. I can't believe how that asshole treated me. I can't believe I ever slept with him. I can't believe—

A car hydroplanes ahead of me and does a three-sixty. My instinct is to slam on my brakes which sends me spinning too because it's the wrong move to make.

I miss the car by mere inches. *WHAM*! I hit the guardrail and my body jars.

Shit! Another SUV slides up behind me, and all I can see are headlights before I'm rocked back and forth as my car jerks and air bags go off. Stars burst in my vision and I can't breathe.

Then time stops.

Chapter 22

Trey

"Where's mom?"

"I don't know, little man." I keep staring out the front window, wondering the same thing. She's been gone a long time. No way is she still picking paint samples out at the store. My girl's too decisive.

Maybe she went for a drive to clear her head?

Shit, I can't believe the day she had. I'm so pissed about her interview and what that cocksucker said to her, that I've spent the better part of an hour imagining all the ways I'd like to kill him. They all involve slow torture, a spoon, and a chainsaw.

I've tried calling Erin's cell twice now, and both times it went to voicemail.

Something's not sitting right with me. What if something's happened to her?

I call her again, and again, I get no answer.
Trey: You okay?
I'm left on delivered.

My chest hurts. I don't like this one bit.

"Can we eat without her?"

"How about you go ahead. I'll sit with you." I ease into a chair and position myself to see out the front window the whole time.

Just as Beetle finishes his third slice of pizza, Glitch's car pulls into the driveway. I'm up and out the door the second I see Erin in his passenger seat. I run to her side and get the door for her. My relief having her home, safe, is short-lived when I see her face. "What happened?"

She winces as she gets out of the car. "I'm fine."

"The fuck you are!" I hold her shoulders and take in every scratch, scrape, and bruise. "If he did this, I'm going to kill him."

"It wasn't him," she says in a low voice.

Beetle comes outside. "Mom?" He runs at her and hugs her middle. "What happened?"

"I was just in an accident, sweetheart, but I'm alright. It looks worse than it really is."

Glitch's eyes are hard, his mouth forming a tight line as he waits for us to all head inside. "She refused to go to the hospital to get checked out."

"I'm fine, Glitch." It sounds like she's said this to him a dozen times on the way home with the tone she's using.

I don't waste another minute to give her comfort. Scooping her into my arms, I head up the porch. "Get the door open for your mama."

Beetle dashes in and holds it open while I carry my girl inside. I place her gently on the sofa then get an ice pack for her head.

Glitch is already laying out the pillow and blankets I used last night. "I don't like this, Er. You need to get checked out. You could have a concussion."

"I just want to be home, Glitch. The EMT checked me out and said I should be good to go."

"He should have taken you to the ER anyway just to be double sure."

She rolls her eyes at him.

"What happened?" I feel like it's the question I'm forever asking. Always the last to know, the only one out of the loop.

"I wrecked my car after someone else wrecked theirs in front of me and then someone else smashed me from behind afterwards. Good news is, no one was really hurt. Bad news is my car is smooshed and the air bags deployed. That's why my face is so fancy."

I'm wrapping my queen in bubble wrap from this day forward.

Beetle sits down next to her and puts his hand on her leg. "You're gonna be okay though, right?"

"I sure am," she says with a smile. It splits her lip more and blood wells.

I scrub my face with both hands and head into the kitchen for an icepack, meds, and whatever else she might need. I feel sick that I wasn't there for her. I should have driven her to the store myself. I should have insisted we stay together. Why didn't she call me?

Glitch comes into the kitchen. "I'm going to head out."

So soon? "Okay."

"She's going to be okay. Even if she's a stubborn mule for not wanting to get checked out at the hospital, it really does look worse than it is. Her car's probably totaled though."

Glitch rubs the back of his neck. "Christ, that must have scared her. She was silent the whole way home."

I bet this accident rattled her in several ways, especially considering how their parents died.

"You know the drill—vomiting, confusion, all that shit, get her to the ER. Drag her by her feet if she protests."

"I heard that!" Erin yells from the couch.

"Good!" Glitch hollers back. Then he tosses me a small smile. "You sure you can handle a woman like her?"

I huff a laugh. "Guess we're about to find out."

Once he leaves, I bring Erin a bag of frozen peas for her face and over the counter generic pain meds I found in a cabinet.

"Beetle, can you grab me some more pillows off my bed, please?"

He races up the steps on a mission.

Crouching down in front of her, I rub her leg, grateful she wasn't more hurt. I wish she'd called me and not Glitch. I know that sounds selfish and dumb, but it's how I feel. "I'm not leaving until I know you're okay." I was supposed to go home tonight.

"I don't want you to leave at all," she says quietly. Then she stares off and I see a tear fall down her cheek.

She wipes it away before I have the chance to do the honor myself.

"I wanted to call you and couldn't remember your number," she says. "Isn't that awful? I don't have your number memorized."

"It's understandable. I don't have yours memorized either. You're saved in my favorite contacts."

"I couldn't find my cell after the crash. I had to use someone else's to call my brother." She pulls the blanket around her more. "I didn't even make it to the damn store for the paint. Now how am I going to change my life around?"

"Change your life around?" I sit down next to her. "Baby, paint isn't going to make life better."

"No. But you do."

Her words catch me off guard. "Do I?"

"Yeah." She tucks her hair behind her ear. "And I don't want this to derail us. I'll be without a car for a while, but I don't want to stop seeing you. I also don't want you to always make the trip to see me. That's not fair either."

I shut her up with a kiss. "I'm not going anywhere unless you want me to, got it? I'll stay if you want. Shit, I'll rent an apartment close by if I have to. Don't worry about how we're going to make the commute to each other."

"For a moment," she says, slowly, thoughtfully, "I thought about moving far away. From here. From… everyone."

"From me?"

She shook her head. "No. Not you. But I did consider taking your brother up on his offer. Even if it means moving to the bay and being several hours from Glitch."

I shake my head. "I don't think that'll fly for him or Beetle."

"What won't fly?" Beetle asks, carrying a stack of pillows. "I wasn't sure how many, so I grabbed all of them."

Erin laughs when he dumps them beside her. "Thanks, buddy."

Not to get off track, I refocus the conversation. "I've been thinking." I place one pillow under her head and readjust her blanket. "How about I hire you?" She's already about to protest when I add, "Hear me out first then you can argue with me about it, okay?"

She pauses. "Yes… Sir."

Fuuuck, this woman better not get me going with that mouth of hers. Now isn't the time.

"I still want to flip houses, but I'm not going to be able to do both my office jobs while living in a house three hours away, hammering floorboards. I planned to do a lot of the demoing myself, but knew I'd also have to hire a general contractor."

My dad's taught me a lot about the construction business.

"How about I just hire you? Think about it. It's close enough for you to drive to. You can make your own hours, which means getting Beetle from school won't be a problem. We don't have to start this project until after summer, which means you'll have a new car by then." Even if I have to buy her one myself. "I can pay you to oversee everything and work your magic."

"I'm not taking handouts, Trey. I appreciate the offer, but no."

"It's not a handout. It's a chance to make a change. It's a chance to make a lot of money, too."

"I know, but I can't just let you pay me to do that."

"Why not? I'd have to pay someone else to do it if you don't. I know my limits, Er, and taking on a project like this, while still maintaining my other jobs and spending time with you guys will put me beyond my max. The last thing I want is to spread myself thin and ruin what matters most to me."

She licks her lips, and I hope that means she's thinking it over.

"I'll buy the house and give you all the money to hire out whoever we need to make the flip happen. You'll be doing me a favor," I say. "I trust you, Erin. Who knows what kind of dumbass I'd end up hiring if you shoot me down."

"There are a lot of dumbasses out there."

"See what I'm saying? Spare me the headache. Take my money and help me."

She frowns again. "I need a job with healthcare, Trey. Flipping houses is great, but not unless I can have healthcare coverage too. I can't do this."

Now isn't the time to propose, no matter how badly I want to. Shit, I'd marry her on the spot, if I thought she'd be cool with it. Then healthcare wouldn't matter because I can put her on my family plan.

But there's more than me and her in this relationship and I've got work to put in with her son if I want to make Erin and Beetle my family. So for now, I say, "I'll pay you enough to cover healthcare on your own."

"That's outrageous!"

"So will the payout, once we start flipping houses." I think I might have her. "Because this isn't a handout. You're going to work and earn every penny I pay you. And when we sell that house, you and I can go in fifty-fifty with the next one if you want. Then we're going to build your business from there."

"*My* business? This isn't my business!"

"It will be." I roll my shoulders back and look down at her. "What do you say? Want to make every realtor in the tristate area's mouths water? I think you're more than up for the challenge, mama."

"And I think *you're* the one with the possible concussion."

I'm not letting her walk away from this opportunity if I can help it. "Give it a try. What's the worst that can happen?" She won't fail. And I won't fail her. If Erin's willing to give it a go, I'm all for supplying her with everything she needs to make this a success. "It's a win-win. We'll spend more time together, make money, and you'll get your dream job interior designing."

"The start up money for something like this is so much." She shakes her head. "Trey, I can't even come close to contributing."

"Your time and expertise are all the contribution you need to make. I'll handle the money aspect." Does this mean she'll say yes? "I can accept that position with Reid. It might make things a little chaotic at first, but the money will more than pay for everything you'll need to see this project to completion. And I can come down on weekends to spend time with you and Beetle. Help lay carpet, smash some walls, whatever needs to be done."

We can do this. Yeah, it'll be crazy for a bit, but Erin's a leader and I'm a work machine. Besides, we've done this long-distance thing for two years if you think about it. And now that we're out in the open with our relationship, and I can come down on weekends or any other time I want to see her, it's a major step up from what we've been doing. It won't feel like we're losing time with each other because with our history, we're actually gaining more time instead.

"Come on, mama. What do you say?"

Erin's thinking about it. Her eyebrows pinch together, and she chews on her lip. "What if it all flops? What if the market crashes or the profit margin is too small, and you don't make your money back?"

"I will. And if I don't, that's a risk I'm more than willing to take. But what if it *doesn't* flop? What if we become the next hot couple on HGTV?"

That earns me a glorious laugh. "Oh my god, you are concussed. Brendan, call 9-1-1, this man's lost his damn mind."

"I think you should do it, Mom."

We both look over at Beetle at the same time and I smile at him. I'm glad he's on my side. "Say that again?"

"I said I think you should do it." He shrugs and grabs the remote. "I mean, what's there to lose? You keep saying you wish you could be like that girl on TV. If Trey can help you, take the help and do it."

Erin's brow furrows. "Why does he make it sound so logical and simple?"

Because it is that logical and simple. When your dream is dead ahead of you, within reach, all you have to do is grab it.

And that's exactly what I do as I take my girl by the shoulders and dip my head to stare into her gorgeous eyes. "Is that a yes, Erin?"

Chapter 23

Erin

Three and a half months later…

I step over the flooring being installed in the living room and head into the kitchen where Trey is. I tap a box on the counter. "Ohhhh, are these the light fixtures?"

"Probably," Trey says, cutting one open with a box cutter. "I can't believe you got all this done since last week!"

"The boys busted their asses. I just barked orders." I hired a crew that I'm super happy with. They're hardworking, down to earth, and fast. They're also in our budget.

This house is going on the market sooner than we originally planned and I'm dying to see the payout. By my estimate, we'll pocket six figures and that's insane to me.

It's also addicting because Trey's already put bids on two other houses in the area. Together, we were able to get more done here than either of us anticipated. He's been pulling long hours at work but was able to negotiate working four days in the office, which means his has longer weekends with us. Beetle's happy as hell about it too. They spend a lot of time together, playing ball in the backyard or getting into video games.

Glitch and Ara come over for dinner often, and Trey helps complete our family beautifully. The excitement I feel when he pulls into my driveway hasn't died down. I doubt it ever will. And he's already made his mind up that he won't stick with his day job past a year if flipping houses takes off. I think he likes this line of work more than he realized he would.

Or maybe it's just spending time with me all day while we break things and rebuild them.

Grabbing the sledgehammer, I start whacking at the tile floor in the kitchen. It's the last room to demo because it took the longest to order materials for.

Wham! I can't tell you how cathartic this is. *Wham*! To beat the shit out of a floor. *Wham*! And watch it crumble at your feet. *Wham*!

One of my crew members comes in and gives me a wide berth as he goes around me to ask Trey something. I stop beating the ground long enough to wipe the sweat off my forehead.

"Gotta watch her, man. She's dangerous with that thing."

"You think that's bad?" Trey laughs. "You should see the damage she does with a baseball bat."

"Very funny, you two." I have a new water heater, by the way. And I now take long, glorious bubble baths every single night even while I'm doing laundry. It's fantastic. "Besides," I grunt, lift the sledgehammer up over my shoulder and slam into the tile again. *Wham!* "That water heater had it coming."

Trey and I spend the better part of the afternoon in the kitchen. The windows are all open, the fall air keeping us cool all day while we bust our asses, and the sun's gone before dinner time. When everyone leaves to go home for the day, he washes his hands and strips out of his shirt.

God, this man is ripped. And all this heavy lifting and extra cardio I give him is definitely not hurting in the abs department. My man is chiseled to perfection.

"Get your sweet ass over here," he says, hooking his finger at me.

"Yes, Sir." I saunter over and start undoing my shorts. I love that we end our workdays together like this.

"You want the window or the wall?"

"Both."

"Greedy little slut."

That I am. He picks me up and kisses me like a starved man with his first meal in ages while carrying me to the wall first. "You've got some nerve wearing these shorts to work."

He says this about everything I wear. I'm pretty sure Trey would get hard seeing me in a potato sack. "Oh yeah?"

"Yeah." He bites my bottom lip and pulls it a little. "Fuck, you drive me nuts when you break shit around here."

"My sledgehammer skills get you all hot and bothered, huh?"

"You have no fucking clue." He sets me down and pulls my shirt over my head. "Every time you bend over, I get a spectacular view of your ass. And your tits jiggle when your hammer hits home."

"How about if your hammer hits home right now?" I fumble with his belt buckle and yank his pants down. "I've been dying for your dick all day."

He fists my hair before shoving me down on my knees.

I. Love. This.

Grabbing his balls, I massage them hard and give them a good tug.

"Shhhhiiiiitttt." He closes his eyes while I suck on the head of his dick. This man rocks my world every damn day. It's nice to know I do the same for him. Before I get too far, he's already hoisting me back onto my feet. "I've waited all day for your pussy. Fuck if I'm waiting a second longer."

I pull a condom from my pocket and wiggle out of my shorts while he slides it on. Then he fingers me and laughs. "God damn, you're soaked."

"I think it's the sledgehammer."

His deep laugh rumbles my ear as he lifts me up against the wall and slides home. This man fills me to the brim and my body accepts it every time. I swear I'm built to get fucked by Trey. I like the idea of being his personal toy. I love when he gets so riled up, he can't hold back anymore and loses control with me. I love how it burns and stretches and makes me detonate.

I love how we are together.

"I love you," I say, clinging to him for dear life.

"I love you, too, Erin." He pulls out and slides back into me, robbing me of breath. "I'm going to love you until I'm dust."

We hit all four walls in the living room, and then he presses me against the sliding backdoor. I'm thrilled that there's a chance neighbors might see, but I doubt they can. It's dark in here.

Trey fucks me until I'm seeing stars. "You take my dick so well."

"You fuck my pussy like you own it."

"I *do* own it."

I watch him slide in out of me. "Flip me over, take me from the back."

"As my queen wishes."

That's the thing about Trey. He treats me like a queen even when he fucks me like a whore. It's amazing.

My tits smash on the glass when he presses me against the window. "You want everyone to see your beautiful body get fucked, Erin?" He kicks my legs wider and angles his dick, pressing it against my pussy. "Yes or no?"

"Yes." And no. I like the idea of it, but Trey knows I don't really want anyone to witness what we do together. I love the idea of almost being caught and nothing past that.

"You like when I fuck your sweet cunt like this?" He shoves into me, and I gasp. "Yes or no?"

"Yes."

"Yes what?" He pulls out and slams home again.

"Yes, Sir."

"That's a good girl."

My body heats with his words. Tucking my arm behind my back, I wiggle my fingers, giving him the signal that I want him to hold on to me.

He laces his hand in mine and fucks me until I'm screaming his name.

"That's right, slut. Come all over my dick."

I do.

Twice.

Afterwards, we head home and I'm so satisfied, I can't even begin to think about all the work we have to get done tomorrow. Glitch took

Beetle for the night. They're going to some anime art show thing with Ara and he won't be back until tomorrow afternoon.

"You head upstairs and take a bath," Trey says, smacking my ass. "I'll start dinner."

"I can make it."

"I know you can. But I like taking care of you."

That's good. I like him taking care of me too.

Taking the steps, two at a time, I run my hands up the freshly painted walls of my house. We had a painting party with Glitch, Ara, Beetle, and Trey about two months ago and I refreshed the entire color palette of my house. I also bought new, darker carpet for the living room. No new couch yet, but I'm fine with that. My ass fits perfectly in the dip it's taken me years to create in the sofa I have.

I stop at the top of the stairs and look at the framed picture of me, Trey, and Brendan from Glitch's wedding. We look like a family. I love that we look like that. I love that we feel like that.

Trey's been a part of my family longer than I let myself realize.

Once I get the tub filled, I pick out a bath bomb from the gigantic basket Trey made me a few weeks ago, and drop one in. It fizzles and leeches out a teal blue color. I light some candles and turn off the lights. Then I slip into the hot bubbles and sigh.

"What bomb this time?" Trey asks as he slips out of his clothes.

"The mermaid one."

"Nice."

I lean forward so he can slide in behind me. I can't believe how well we fit together. Even in this small bathtub, we manage to make it work.

"What's going through your head, Erin?"

"How do you know I'm thinking about anything?"

"Smoke billows out of your ears."

I laugh against his chest. "I was just thinking about how we fit so perfectly together."

"That we do, baby. That. We. Do."

We spend the night eating Chinese takeout—because he totally cheated and ordered it so he could spend bubble bath time with me instead of cooking—and the rest of the night I laid in his arms, dreaming about what life with Trey will be like.

My future's so bright, my heart is so full, and my family is now perfect.

Epilogue

Trey

One year later…

Erin pats her pumpkin. "I can't wait to carve this baby up."

"You're a very violent woman."

"You knew that when you met me. Remember the turkey?"

"How can I ever forget? I think you stabbing that thing and cussing it out for being too dry was when I started crushing on you."

Erin's house is kitted out with enough spider webs and bloody appendages to stock a movie set. Thanks to a timer, it comes to life every night at seven o'clock and is hands down the spookiest home on the block. The inside looks like a haunted house she should charge people to tour. My girl takes this holiday seriously.

Very. Seriously.

As I lay out various carving knifes and bowls on the dining table, Glitch sets a huge pumpkin at each seat. "I'm winning the carving contest this year."

This is an annual tradition.

I cock my eyebrow. "Says who?"

"Says the defending champion from last year." Glitch takes one of the larger knives and stabs his pumpkin through the top.

"I bet Trey's going to win this time." Erin hands a spoon to Beetle. "What do you think, kiddo?"

"Nope. It's gonna be me." Beetle waits for Erin to cut off the top of his big pumpkin. "I have the best idea this year."

"I can't wait to see it!" Erin ruffles his hair. "Put all your seeds in the green bowl. I'll roast them for a snack later when we start the horror movie." She carves into the pumpkin with no mercy and rips the top off. "There you go, buddy. Gut it."

I watch, fascinated, as Erin makes quick work of her own pumpkin next. Instead of using a spoon to scoop the seeds out, she always uses her hands. "You're still a monster, I see."

She leans over and whispers, "Maybe after you're done rearranging your pumpkin's guts, you'll take me upstairs and rearrange mine."

God, I love this woman.

We start dumping our seeds into the huge bowl and halfway through carving our masterpieces, Erin goes into the kitchen and grabs a few more beers. Halloween songs play in the living room and Ara dances while she paints her pumpkin instead of carving it.

I love that we do this every year.

Looking over at Glitch, I see he's working in secret with an entire container of toothpicks. He glances up when he senses me staring at him. "No peeking."

"The hell you doing with all those toothpicks, man?"

He shrugs and keeps working on his carving. "It's part of my method."

Doesn't surprise me. With the time and care he puts into everything else I have no doubt he'll be the champion of the carving contest tonight. He's won the last three years in a row, fucker.

But he's not the only one working in secret. We all are. No one can look at anyone else's carving until the very end when we're all finished and do a big reveal. Then it goes to a vote. Winner gets to pick the horror movie.

We're an hour into carving when Erin finally puts down her knife and sighs, "Well, I'm done."

Beetle looks up from his pumpkin. "Can you start roasting the seeds now?"

"Sure!" She's in the best mood tonight and I love seeing her so happy. I think she looks forward to this contest every year the most.

Once Erin grabs the bowl of seeds, there's a collective pause as she walks away with it.

I look at Beetle, then Glitch, then Ara. They're all staring back at me.

My heart's in my goddamn throat.

I hear the water running and a cabinet door closing with a thud. My hearing becomes so acute, the sound of all the seeds pouring into what I assume is a colander is loud in my ears. Then the water shuts off.

I think I might pass out.

Erin walks, ever so slowly, back into the dining room, holding what I'd snuck into the bowl of seeds an hour ago when she refreshed our drinks.

"What… what is this?"

The silence in the room is as loud as a scream.

"Trey?" She walks over to me, and I see her hands are shaking.

I get up and close the distance between us. Then I go down on one knee.

Taking the small box from her trembling hands, I open it to reveal a ring. "Erin…"

She cups her mouth, her eyes huge and teary. She's got pumpkin stuck to her fingers and her nails are stained orange.

My beautiful, chaotic, fierce queen.

On cue, everyone turns their pumpkins around to face her.

Beetle's says "**Will You**"

Glitch's says, "**Marry Me?**"

Ara's says, "**Yes or No.**"

Her knees start to wobble, and she bursts into tears.

Holy shit, I hope they're happy tears.

I asked Beetle permission to ask for Erin's hand in marriage last night and talked with Glitch about it this morning. They were both so happy, I didn't think twice about this being a flop. But now, Erin's got me worried.

She just keeps crying.

"Yes or No, Mom."

I look over at Beetle, and, fuck, his cheeks are turning red. He's as nervous as me and I'm sure seeing his mother cry is messing with his emotions.

Erin steps back from me.

I hold my breath.

Instead of taking the paintbrush Ara's holding out for her, she grabs a knife instead.

Then she walks over to Ara's pumpkin and starts carving for what feels like ages.

She won't let anyone see it.

I'm still on my goddamn knees.

Letting out a long exhale, she locks gazes with me and spins the pumpkin around with her answer.

YES has a heart carved around it.

"Yes?" I stand up and rush to her. "You're saying Yes?!"

"YES!"

I scoop Erin into my arms and spin her around in circles. "I promise I'm going to make you and Beetle so happy."

"You already do." She smashes her mouth to mine and kisses the soul right out of me.

I set her down and we turn to face everyone. "Well, looks like I get to pick the horror movie tonight." Because clearly I'm the winner. I turn my pumpkin around and let her see what I've carved.

I love you, FLIP.

Erin gawks at it. "FLIP? You're calling me Flip now?"

"You flip your shit, you flip houses, and you flip off everyone who pisses you off." I cup her face and kiss her again. "It suits you."

Besides, she has nicknames for everyone else—mine can't be used in public, by the way—so I think she deserves to have one too.

"Flip," Ara says. "I like it!"

Glitch laughs, his deep rumbling voice hitting us all in the chest. "It does suit you, Er."

She proves my point by flipping her brother off.

"Hey!" He tosses a hunk of pumpkin at her. "Beetle's in the room!"

Erin flips Glitch off with both middle fingers this time. Then she grabs her son and hugs him tight. "You knew about all this, huh?"

"Yup. I helped pick the ring out."

This is the happiest day of my life and as I sit at the stained dining room table with pumpkin chunks, slimy seeds, and paint scattered across it, I can't imagine a better place to be. Her family has been part of mine for so long, it's like we've always been together.

"Hey, can I go to Jackson's sleepover now?"

Erin's brow furrows. "Now? I thought we agreed you could go to his sleepover after our family night. It's only six o'clock!"

"*Mom.*"

"But what about the movie? The snacks?"

"We *always* do horror movies and snacks. I have all the best ones memorized anyway. Please, can I go to Jackson's now?"

"I'll take him," Glitch says. "We're going to hit the road too."

"But…" Erin looks at each of them like they just took away all her toys.

"I'm sure you'll find something to occupy your night with," Ara says with a wink.

Erin doesn't even try to hide her smile. Her attitude flips so fast she goes from disappointed to excited in a blink. "Right. Okay, yes, you can totally go to Jackson's now but I'm picking you up at nine am sharp because we have to go see a new house we might put a bid on and you've got soccer."

I kiss her neck and wrap my arms around her middle. "I'll hold her back, you guys run! Save yourselves!"

Beetle cackle-laughs as he races out of the house. The boy doesn't even grab his overnight bag.

Glitch picks it up off the floor and gives me a salute. "Have fun, you two."

Ara giggles when he smacks her ass as she walks out.

The door closes, and suddenly it's just the two of us.

The way we can go from chaos to calm in a blink is wild. I love it.

"So," Erin says, tugging my hand. "About that promise you made me."

"Promise? What promise?" I let her lead me out of the dining room and up the stairs.

"The one about wearing the Ghostface mask and making me scream while I come around your big dick."

Ohhhh *that* promise.

I stalk after her. "Well, I don't break promises now, do I?"

"Nope." Her face lights up and she dashes into the bedroom with me hot on her heels.

"Get on your knees, dirty girl." I pull off my shirt and toss it to the floor. "I want you to scream my name until all the neighbors know who you belong to."

I slide on the mask and make good on my promise.

*Want to read a bonus scene of Glitch and Ara's wedding from their point of view? Go to www.BrianaMichaels.com and click on Bonus Content. Don't forget to join my newsletter too!

Other Books By This Author

Hell Hounds Harem Series:
Restless Spirit
The Dark Truth
The Devil's Darling
Hard To Find
Hard To Love
Hard To Kill
Raise Hell
Raise the Dead
Ruler of the Righteous

Sins of the Sidhe Series:
Shatter
Shine
Passion
Bargains
Ignite
Awaken
Rise
Exile
Discord

The Reflection Series:
Burn for Her
Lured by Her
Struck by Her

Contemporary:
Glitch
Flip

For information on this book and other future releases, please visit my website: www.BrianaMichaels.com

If you liked this book, please help spread the word by leaving a review on the site you purchased your copy, or on a reader site such as Goodreads.

I'd love to hear from readers too, so feel free to send me an email at: sinsofthesidhe@gmail.com or visit me on Facebook: www.facebook.com/BrianaMichaelsAuthor

About the Author

Briana Michaels grew up and still lives on the East Coast. When taking a break from the crazy adventures in her head, she enjoys running around with her two children. If there is time to spare, she loves to read, cook, hike in the woods, and sit outside by a roaring fire. She does all of this with the love and support of her amazing husband who always has her back, encouraging her to go for her dreams.